ATTACK OF THE KILLER KOMODOS

ALSO BY SUMMER RACHEL SHORT

The Mutant Mushroom Takeover

ATTACK
OF THE
KILLER
KOMODOS

A MAGGIE AND NATE MYSTERY

Summer Rachel Short

Simon & Schuster Books for Young Readers
NEW YORK   LONDON   TORONTO   SYDNEY   NEW DELHI

SIMON & SCHUSTER BOOKS FOR YOUNG READERS
An imprint of Simon & Schuster Children's Publishing Division
1230 Avenue of the Americas, New York, New York 10020
SIMON & SCHUSTER BOOKS FOR YOUNG READERS
and related marks are trademarks of Simon & Schuster, Inc.
For information about special discounts for bulk purchases, please contact Simon & Schuster
Special Sales at 1-866-506-1949 or business@simonandschuster.com.
The Simon & Schuster Speakers Bureau can bring authors to your live event.
For more information or to book an event, contact the Simon & Schuster Speakers Bureau at
1-866-248-3049 or visit our website at www.simonspeakers.com.
Interior design by Hilary Zarycky
The text for this book was set in Adobe Caslon Pro.
Manufactured in the United States of America
0821 FFG
First Edition
2 4 6 8 10 9 7 5 3 1
CIP data for this book is available from the Library of Congress.
ISBN 9781534468689
ISBN 9781534468702 (eBook)

"In every walk with nature one receives far more than he seeks."
—*John Muir*

ATTACK
OF THE
KILLER
KOMODOS

CHAPTER ONE

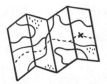

Water the color of bullfrogs gurgles against my shins as we slog across the Firehole River. Nate swings a rope in an unruly figure eight and bellows a Bigfoot call that sounds like a dying whoopee cushion sputtering out its final serenade.

I zoom in the video camera as he takes a wobbly step toward the riverbank. The smell of pine sap and spicy sagebrush mingles with my SPF 75 and citronella bug spray.

We've been in Yellowstone National Park less than twenty-four hours, and we're already on the hunt for the legendary primate. As an up-and-coming naturalist, I'm skeptical about the big guy's existence, but humoring Nate is number three on my Yellowstone Vacation Bucket List. Plus, hanging out in the wilds of the park is basically my definition of paradise.

"You getting all this, Mags?" Nate calls over his shoulder. He's got on dark shades and a few streaks of black paint spread across his freckled cheeks, plus a neon green

I BELIEVE T-shirt that pretty much cancels out the camo face paint. "Make sure you get a close-up of the mini grappling hook."

"Already on it, partner," I say, giving him a thumbs-up. I've recently signed on as the production manager for Nate's YouTube channel, *The Conspiracy Squad*. The pay is squat, and the working conditions are questionable. But investigating the unexplained is kinda our thing, though Nate's tastes run more to the otherworldly than mine. The show's dedicated to freaky, weird, and potentially made-up happenings. It used to be small potatoes, but ever since a mutated zombie fungus spread through our hometown six weeks ago, *The Conspiracy Squad* has been getting more attention. Nate's even had a couple of companies reach out to him looking to sponsor segments, hence the rope and grappling hook. My latest contribution to the show is a segment I've dubbed "Maggie's Minute." At the end of each episode, I give a few tidbits that offer a scientific explanation for whatever paranormal finding Nate's reporting on. He even made me some cool intro music. Fans seem to dig it. Though I do get a lot of questions about the Bermuda Triangle and the Lost City of Atlantis. I haven't come up with good explanations for those just yet. But the world's full of mysteries. Like sand dunes that make songs that sound like chanting monks or the way birds can find their way home after traveling thousands of miles without ever using a map or GPS.

I record another minute of Nate stomping around and belching out grunts that sound more like indigestion than primate calls. I glance up from the camcorder. "You might wanna go easy on the sound effects if you really want a shot at attracting an elusive species."

"Lots of Squatchers have tried that route and got diddly to show for it. My strategy is to go in loud and proud. Let the hairy dude know I mean business." Nate whirls in a dramatic spin, his rope high, like an eleven-year-old mythical beast wrangler.

As I wipe a spray of river water from the camera's screen, my stomach rumbles and I think about Dad back at the campsite grilling up lunch. This week's going to be our first chance in a long while to really kick back and spend some time together. He's promised me a hike this afternoon and marshmallow roasting over the campfire after that—numbers one and two on the bucket list.

Nate suddenly stops gyrating and points to a scattering of evergreens along the riverbank. "Mags," he hisses. "I think there might really be something out here."

"It's probably just a squirrel or a muskrat," I say, but narrow my eyes and scan the tree line anyway. Lately, disaster has a way of sniffing us out quicker than a gang of mosquitoes on a sticky summer's night.

Nate edges to the shore. "If my gut's singing the tune

I think it is, this just might be our big breakthrough."

Nate's gut is notoriously unpredictable. Especially after half a bag of Flamin' Hot Cheezy Poppers. The sagebrush rustles, and a cloud of dust puffs out. My heart hiccups. I'm not expecting Bigfoot, but Yellowstone's got a few real-deal hazards. Before we piled into Gramma's Ford for the fifteen-hundred-mile trip out to visit Dad, I did loads of research. Thermal pools brimming with scalding-hot water. Territorial moose and grumpy bison. Packs of roaming wolves. And the head honcho of the Yellowstone predators, the grizzly.

"Careful, Nate. We don't want a run-in with a mama bear."

Nate ignores me and tiptoes closer. "All the urban legends say Bigfoot hangs out near food and water. We've got the river, and there's a load of half-munched berries on the ground." He pauses and sniffs. "Yeti B.O."

I skid up to the shore, water slopping out the sides of my sneakers. "Don't go stirring anything up until I get there!"

"This dude reeks!" Nate pokes his toe into a clump of prickly brush.

I sniff. "I don't think that's a Bigfoot. That smells like—"

"Skunk!" Nate scrambles back as a black-and-white tail emerges from the sage.

A skunk is better than a grizzly, but not by much. I

shove the video camera into my backpack and thrust my nose into my T-shirt. "Gramma's gonna kill me if we come back to the campground stinking like skunk rump."

The tail scoots forward, but no fluffy rodent body follows. Instead, a hulking reptile emerges, skunk tail clasped between its scaly jaws. The lizard swoops toward Nate with a clumsy, swishing trot.

"Get back!" I snatch a branch off the ground. The lizard spits out the skunk's severed tail but keeps charging our way. A long, yellow tongue with a distinct fork swishes out of its mouth.

"You never told me Yellowstone had baby Godzillas!" Nate backpedals from the beady-eyed giant.

The lizard's as long as an alligator and has to weigh a few hundred pounds. Stringy saliva drips from its jowls. This thing shouldn't be here. The Yellowstone guidebook I read on the way up said the park only had one species of lizard. A tiny, bug-eating critter that could fit in the palm of my hand.

This thing is in a whole other league.

Massive. Foul drool. Definitely carnivorous. I wrack my brain trying to remember all the research I did about lizards back when I bought my pet leopard gecko. Only one lizard fits the bill, and it's native to Indonesia. "It's a Komodo dragon," I breathe.

Nate's eyes go wide, and I can practically hear the

conspiracy theories bubbling around in his skull. "Did you just confirm the existence of dragons? Because if you did—" Nate stumbles over the rope's grappling hook and crashes to the ground, his flip-flop soaring into the air.

I thrust my arm out to Nate. "They don't breathe fire or fly. But they're fast and have huge appetites."

The Komodo dragon whips forward and sinks its slimy teeth into Nate's sandal.

Nate grips my arm and leaps to his feet. We bolt, abandoning the rope and Nate's flip-flop.

"How'd that thing get here?" Nate pants as we turn around and slosh back through the river. "Somebody's pet get loose?"

"Nobody in their right mind would keep a Komodo dragon as a pet. Their bites are loaded with venom that causes their victims to die a slow, gruesome death."

Nate peers back at where we left the hulking reptile. "Maybe we could save the nature lesson for later, Mags."

I follow his gaze. A long, dark form swishes into the river after us.

"There's one more thing," I call as we break into a watery sprint. "Komodo dragons are fantastic swimmers."

CHAPTER TWO

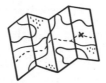

The dragon disappears under the swirling green water. We scramble through the river faster and are nearly to the opposite shore when Nate shrieks and crumples down with a splash. He stretches out one arm. "Run, Mags! It's chomping me up whole!"

I drop to my hands and knees. Cold water spills over my shorts. I scoop up a rock and scan the river, ready to pelt the scaly fiend if I have to. But instead of razor-sharp teeth piercing Nate's leg, there's a tangle of weeds wrapped around his ankle in a slippery, green knot. I drop the rock and tear away the plants. "You're okay," I say, my pulse sliding back down to nearly normal.

"False alarm." Nate gives a sheepish smile.

Just then the river erupts as the Komodo dragon thrashes up.

"Ahhhhh!" We scream and spring to our feet.

Water flies off the lizard as it jerks its head from side to side, a rainbow trout wriggling in its jaws.

We go into full-blown cheetah mode, not stopping until we reach the shore. My gaze dashes back to the dragon. It still lingers in the middle of the river. Its black eyes have a feisty look in them that reminds me of my pet gecko when he's munching live crickets.

It flicks out its tongue like it's a connoisseur of fine prey and we're the next course. "Most reptiles only attack when they're hungry or scared. But this one sinks its teeth into everything that strolls its way," I pant.

"This is just like issue 414 of *Midnight Kingdom*, where Brigadier Ajax fought a mechanical piranha warlord. The dude ate Ajax's entire army in a single night. It was brutal." Nate eyes the dragon like a wizened general who's seen one too many battles.

At last, the Komodo swallows down the fish and swishes toward the far riverbank. As it crawls onto land, its back legs emerge from the water. The sun glints off something metallic wrapped around one ankle. I nudge Nate. "Check it out. It's got a tag."

Nate squints. "What does that mean? That the dragon really is a pet?"

"It looks more like the kind of thing scientists use to track wildlife."

"Well, whoever is supposed to be keeping tabs on Captain BiteyPants is majorly blowing it."

I can't argue with that. On top of the lizard being supersized and extra cranky, it's also a long way from home. As the lizard crawls back to the sagebrush, it lowers its neck and picks up something black and white. I squint. It's the grody skunk tail. Clumps of fur fly from the Komodo's mouth as it gulps down the remains.

"Seriously?" Nate shakes his head. "Does that thing ever quit pounding down grub?"

"Let's hope so. The last thing the park needs is an invasive predator shaking things up. We'll fill Dad in as soon as we get back to the campground. He'll know what to do."

Up until six months ago, Dad lived with us in Shady Pines, Texas, but after a big mix-up at his old job, he got fired. He couldn't find a local job and ended up moving out to Yellowstone to work as a park ranger. Having Dad live over a thousand miles away is pretty much the worst, but I've already tried fixing things on my own, and that ended up being a huge disaster. So for now I'm trying to be patient and hope things will work themselves out.

Nate arches a brow. "You sure we can trust your dad with this kinda news?"

I roll my eyes. "Not this again." Before we left for Yellowstone, Nate watched some far-fetched documentary claiming there's a conspiracy among park rangers to keep Bigfoot and other urban legends a secret. Now he's convinced Dad's got the inside scoop on Sasquatch. "Dad isn't involved with any conspiracy, and he definitely isn't hiding Bigfoot."

Nate grunts. "According to the documentary, it's always the people you least suspect."

I sigh. Trying to convince Nate to see things from a scientific point of view is a losing battle. "Let's just get to my dad."

Nate frowns. "Once we tell him, that'll be the end of it. My one shot at being a real-deal dragon hunter gone just like that."

"Not a real dragon, remember?"

"Fine, but if that dragon—not to be confused with the mythical, treasure-stealing kind—isn't local, and it isn't somebody's pet, how'd it get here?" Nate asks.

I grip my T-shirt and wring out river water. I've been asking myself the same question. "I don't know. But however it happened, it's not good."

On our way back to the campsite, the forest's dark canopy casts long shadows. I sneak a glance over my shoulder, just to be sure nothing scaly is lurking behind us.

Nate lifts his ball cap and runs a hand through his heap of curls. "You didn't happen to catch any of that on camera, did you?"

"I was kinda trying to avoid having my appendages devoured."

"Understandable," Nate says, flopping through the

woods with one bare foot. "Maybe we could re-create the moment back home with your gecko and some super zoomed-in shots. . . ."

Nate's voice drifts off, and he gets a faraway look in his eye, like he's dreaming up an epic scheme. I flash back to a million different adventures we've had over the years. Building the world's greatest treehouse, aka Headquarters, using nothing but scrap wood and discarded odds and ends. Biking the backroads of Shady Pines in search of crop circles. And most recently, saving my brother and the rest of the town from a deadly mutant fungus. Nate and I may not always see things the same way, but somehow we bring out the best in each other anyhow.

Our campsite comes into view—extra-large family tent, a circle of chairs around the campfire, and a bag of food hanging on a pole eight feet high to keep the bears away. Daisy, the yellow mare Dad uses to get around the back county, swishes her tail and gives a low whinny. Before we make it to the tent, I spot my thirteen-year-old brother, Ezra, standing too close to a tree, eyes locked on something small and dark.

"Everything all right?" I ask as the dark thing twitches.

"Not unless you call being injured and majorly outnumbered all right," Ezra answers, and stretches out one hand toward the tree.

I take a closer look. A two-inch cockroach is surrounded

by a squad of army ants. I bite my lip. Ever since the fungus invasion, Ezra's been on a mission to save every creepy crawly creature he comes across. That is, when he's not zoned out, staring into space. The cockroach limps and makes a disturbing buzzing sound. "Maybe you should just let nature take its course. Just this once."

Ezra turns to face me, his dark eyes wide. "What if you'd just let nature take its course with me?"

"That was different. You're not a cockroach."

Ezra shakes his head. "I'm helping this guy. End of story."

Nate peeks at the roach and makes a gagging face.

I take a step back. "Have you seen Dad lately? I need to talk to him."

The cockroach creeps onto Ezra's open palm. "Check the tent."

I head that way and am about to unzip the canvas door when I hear hushed voices coming from inside.

"That sounds like a whole mess of trouble, Tommy. You remember what happened back in Shady Pines. You don't want to end up fired again," I hear Gramma say.

"Don't worry, Mom. I've got it all under control. I'm not gonna lose my job," Dad answers.

"From my experience, people always think they've got things under control until they're wrapped up in some big, nasty disaster. If you want my advice, let the thing be somebody else's problem. You've got the kids to think of," Gramma replies. "Somebody could get hurt, and that somebody just might be you."

Dad sighs. "You worry too much."

Before I can decide whether to keep eavesdropping or yank down the zipper and get to the bottom of whatever Gramma and Dad are talking about, there's rustling and the sound of footsteps coming my way. I scramble from the tent and race back to Ezra and Nate. Sweat pricks along my forehead and my head swims. Dad is supposed to be spending quality time with me and Ezra this week, not getting himself tangled up in dangerous shenanigans.

"That was fast," Nate says, looking gloomy. "I guess your dad's gonna zip outta here and capture the thing all Indiana Jones–like."

"I didn't actually tell him about the Komodo yet." I glance over my shoulder, wondering what Dad could possibly be up to that might risk his job.

Nate grins. "You won't regret this. We're gonna get the most killer video ever."

Before I can answer Nate, the tent flap opens. Dad looks around the campsite, spots us, and waves. A twirl of smoke drifts over the camp chairs. Dad makes a sudden beeline for the fire. He grabs a skewer and pokes a blackened hunk. Ash tumbles out of the flames, streaking Dad's gray park ranger shirt and avocado-green pants with soot.

He shakes his head and calls, "These hot dogs aren't looking so good. How do you kiddos feel about ramen and Vienna sausages?"

"Over my dead body." Gramma saunters out of the tent. She's wearing a fuchsia tracksuit and a hefty polka-dot fanny pack. It's what Gramma calls an "outdoorsy" look, but with her silvery hair sprayed into spikes and ginormous gold hoop earrings, she looks ready to walk the Thurston County Outlet Mall, not spend a week in a national park.

Gramma smirks when she catches sight of me and Nate. "You two been mud wrestling some wild boars?"

Nate shoots me a sideways glance. "Just snagging footage for *The Conspiracy Squad*, ma'am."

"Probably tricky to get good video out this way. From what I hear, UFOs hate paying the park entrance fees." Dad chuckles.

Nate tips his ball cap. "Not too shabby, Mr. Stone. I, for one, appreciate a solid dad joke from time to time."

I try to add a little laugh, but only part of me is listening. I need to know the scoop on what's up with Dad.

"I'm riding out to the camp store," Gramma announces, reaching for a wide-seat bicycle with a bell and basket between the handlebars. "I'm making campfire turkey tetrazzini, garlic bread, and caramel brownie pie for supper."

Nate clutches his belly and gives a longing sigh. "Your words are sweet, sweet music to my hollow innards."

"You sure you're up for the ride?" Dad asks. "It's at least five miles to the parking lot."

"Piece of cake." Gramma sniffs. "I've been doing Jazzercize on home video since Christmas. I'm probably the fittest one of this bunch."

"All right, then. Happy riding," Dad says.

Gramma rings the bell and gives a wave.

"While we're waiting on something other than canned meat, what do you kids say we take that hike I promised?" Dad asks. "There's a fumarole about a mile from here."

"Fumarole?" Nate asks. "As in fumes. As in this is gonna be Stink City?"

"On a scale of one to garbage dump, I'd say we're looking at a solid five," Dad answers. "But it'll be worth it. Yellowstone's world famous for its hydrothermal features— geysers, mud pots, hot springs."

I glance at the tent and bite my lip. Twenty minutes ago, I was totally jazzed about the prospect of a nature hike, but now all I can think about is some nameless trouble lurking just around the corner. "I need to change my clothes first. We got wet in the river."

"Sure thing," Dad says with a smile.

I study his face, trying to decide whether that's his usual grin or if there's something a little off about it. I think I notice a twinge of worry around his eyes, but it might just be a squint from the sun.

Nate kicks off his lone flip-flop and grabs a pair of sneakers. "We passing by any grassy spots on the way? Jackalopes love grass."

Dad pops on his park ranger hat. "You're talking about the little bunnies with antlers? I've seen a lot of critters around the park, but I'm afraid jackalopes aren't one of them."

Nate waves a hand, looking completely unfazed. "No offense, Mr. Stone, but you gotta have a certain vibe to attract legendary creatures. They can sniff out skeptics from a mile away."

CHAPTER THREE

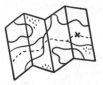

zip up the door, change into dry clothes, then peer around the tent. I spot my journal on my cot. It's filled with nature sketches, notes on scientific findings from around Shady Pines, a few new entries on things I've spotted in Yellowstone, and of course, my bucket list. I cross the tent to grab the journal and make a note about the Komodo, when I notice Dad's duffel bag is partially unzipped. Something shiny catches the sunlight streaming in through the tent's thin walls. I kneel and push Dad's jacket to the side. My fingers bump into cold metal.

"What's taking so long, Mags?" Ezra calls from outside the tent. "I want my earbuds."

I ignore Ezra and lift the object out of the bag. My breath catches. It's a silver band . . . just like the one we saw on the Komodo dragon's ankle. I roll it over in my hand. On the inside of the metal, there's a small button battery and what looks like a tiny antennae. I flick the thin metal strand. There could be lots of explanations for this.

Dad's a park ranger. He probably tracks plenty of animals. Animals that aren't rogue Komodo dragons. But Gramma said whatever he was involved in might be dangerous. A hulking reptilian predator is like the definition of dangerous. I tuck the band back in Dad's duffel and zip it up tight. "Coming!" I call back.

Ten minutes later, Dad, Nate, and I are hiking along a winding trail through a golden meadow sprinkled with violet and powder-pink wildflowers. Ezra said he wanted to stay behind and take a nap. Even though he slept in until nearly noon today. I really thought coming out to Yellowstone and seeing Dad again might help him snap out of the funk he's been in after everything went down back home. But so far, it hasn't changed anything.

A herd of bison grazes in the distance. Their heads are humongous and shaggy with beards of dark brown fur. They remind me of bulls, only instead of seeming like hotheads they've got a wild, carefree sort of vibe.

As the path curves, we pass under an aspen tree. Dad stops and holds a finger to his lips. A bright yellow bird perches on a branch. "It's a male American goldfinch," he whispers.

The goldfinch tilts its tiny black-and-yellow face to one side as if saying hello to us all. The bird is beautiful and normally I'd want to whip out my journal and sketch it, but my eyes seem to stare straight through it. I can't stop wondering if there's a connection between the silver band in the duffel bag, the Komodo dragon, and Dad's talk with Gramma. Dad wouldn't intentionally release a dangerous reptile into the park. But he's quirky. What if he'd been testing out some new reptile theory and then things went wonky and the next thing he knew the lizard was on the loose? I gnaw on my bottom lip. But then again if Dad knows about the Komodo dragon, wouldn't he be going after it right now instead of taking us on a hike?

Gurgles drift through the air. "We're passing the Firehole River now. The fumarole's just around this bend. You guys are in for a treat," Dad says with a little extra pep in his step.

We come to a stop. Suddenly I feel like I've been transported to another world. Waves of swirling fog churn up from an opening in the rocky ground. There's a hissing sound as the clouds twist and roll out like smoke from a chimney. Nearby, there's a thermal pool ringed with bright colors—crimson, sunset orange, and emerald green. In the center, the water is the brightest blue I've ever seen and looks so deep you could dive in and never reach the bottom.

Nate rubs his palms together. "What are we waiting for? Let's get over there. I've got an idea for a killer shot."

"Killer is right," Dad says. "Those pools are sulfuric stews of boiling chemicals. Every winter, some animal gets too close and falls in. Never to be seen again."

Dad hands me his binoculars and I focus them on the thermal pool's color rings. As the fog drifts closer, a smell like rotten eggs slinks through the air.

Nate sniffs. "Okay, I'm just gonna go ahead and say it now. That's not me."

Dad points to a curl of steam rising from the earth. "That's actually Yellowstone's trademark scent. It's from the sulfuric acid in the pools."

I shift the binoculars toward a twisting plume. The cloud grows wider and taller, like a pressure cooker building steam. Finally, a storm-size cloud of white puffs out, filling the air with even more stink.

"Impressive," Nate says. "For nature, anyway."

"If you like that, wait until you get a look at Old Faithful. It blasts over a hundred feet. And not just steam, but thousands of gallons of water each time it erupts." Dad slides his hands into his pockets, looking totally calm and happy.

Nate strokes his chin. "So does Yellowstone have like a giant broken water pipe underground, or does it just like belching out stank all over the place?"

Dad laughs. "That's not a bad theory, but Yellowstone actually sits on a super volcano, maybe the largest in the world. Rivers of magma are flowing under our feet."

"In issue 129 of *Midnight Kingdom*, Planet Saluthia

had rivers of magma. It also had sentient fire leeches. They were mega-tough."

"No fire leeches around here," Dad says. "But the magma does give Yellowstone its geysers, mud pots, and fumaroles. That, and it plays a role in some of the earthquakes the park experiences."

Nate taps the tips of his fingers together, considering. "A mondo earthquake would make a pretty epic video. But I don't think I'd like to get tossed all over the place by some traitorous patch of dirt."

"The park gets a couple thousand quakes every year, but most of them are so small you'd never even feel them. Only every now and then are they more serious. One of the worst in the area was a 7.2 on the moment magnitude scale. Geysers formed, and a whole new lake came into existence. There were aftershocks and swarms for days," Dad says.

"Swarms? I thought we were talking earthquakes, not bees," Nate says.

"Aftershocks are the quakes that come after a big seismic event, and earthquake swarms are little quakes that happen in one area over a short amount of time. Yellowstone sometimes gets both," Dad answers.

Nate's eyes bug out. "And people think this is a good spot for a vacay?"

"The real hazards are getting too close to thermal

features or wild animals. Avoid those and you've got nothing to worry about," Dad answers.

I start to lower the binoculars but notice a grassy heap the size of a beanbag chair at the edge of the thermal pool. I adjust the focus. The pile has a pitted center with a load of five large eggs. "Whoa."

Dad leans over. "What do you see, Mags?"

I hand him the binocs and point to the heap.

He adjusts the focus. "It looks like a sandhill crane nest. But they usually only lay two eggs and not that close to hot water."

Steam drifts off the surface of the pool and swirls around the nest. "How long till they hatch?" Nate asks. "Some eggs cracking might fit in good with a *Conspiracy Squad* segment I'm planning on feathered extraterrestrials."

"Unfortunately, these guys don't stand a chance that close to the heat." Dad gazes out at the fumarole for a long minute, then adds, "Oh, look, we're getting an encore."

Nate pulls out his camera and films the scene providing a mini-monologue about how the sputtering fumarole is the blowhole of a gigantic thermonuclear marine mammal. Another big puff of steam swells out, making everything so foggy that it's hard to see more than a few feet away. Nate gags and tucks his camera in his bag. "Sorry, but I can't handle any more of nature's stink. I'll meet you back in the fresh air zone."

Nate takes off, and Dad and I stand without speaking. A whisper of mist sweeps up from the pool. I tug at the bottom of my ponytail, trying to work out the perfect question to get Dad to spill his guts, but nothing clever comes to mind so instead I go with the facts. "Nate and I saw a Komodo dragon at the river. It ate Nate's flip-flop . . . and a skunk tail."

Dad blinks. "And you're just now telling me about it?"

"I was going to say something earlier . . . but then I got distracted." I consider telling him that I overheard his talk with Gramma and that I found the tracking bracelet in his bag, but then Dad lifts off his hat and pushes his hands through his hair. He suddenly looks much less relaxed.

"Komodo dragons don't live in Yellowstone, Maggie," he says.

"I know, and a new predator in the park could be a serious problem. It was pounding down grub left and right."

Dad doesn't answer right away, and my stomach churns. I can't decide whether he's being cautious or if he just doesn't believe me. I swallow hard and add, "The lizard had a band around its ankle. The kind scientists put on animals they're tracking."

Something shifts in Dad's eyes and he suddenly looks more alert. "You're sure about that?"

"Hundred percent." I bob my chin up and down.

Dad looks to the fumarole. It sputters and wafts misty

clouds over the trail. When he turns back to me, he stands up stiff and straight. His face is all businesslike. "I want you kids to stay away from the river until I've had a chance to check things out. Understand?"

"Okay, sure," I say. "Are you going after it? If you are, you should probably call in some backup. That thing was big and hungry and extra grumpy."

"I'll be fine," he answers with a quick smile and a dismissive wave that doesn't make me feel any better about the situation.

"Dad, is everything okay?" I dig the toe of my sneaker into the dirt. "I sort of heard you and Gramma talking earlier. She sounded worried about you . . . she thought you might lose your job?"

His smile slowly fades, and I wish I hadn't brought up that last part. "You don't need to worry, Mags. I'm just keeping an eye on some things in the park. I'm not going to get fired."

Maybe I should stop asking questions now. I don't like upsetting Dad, but the not knowing keeps gnawing at me and I can't seem to stay quiet. "What kind of things are you looking into?"

Dad sighs. "You kids are curious . . . and I love that. But in a place like Yellowstone, curiosity can get you hurt. I just need you to trust that I've got it under control. Can you do that for me?"

I give a slight nod.

"It'll all work out," he says, and pats my shoulder, then glances toward the dying fumarole. "Well, I guess we'd better start heading back."

As he sets off on the trail ahead of me, I remember the conspiracy documentary Nate told me about. The one with park rangers keeping secrets from their family and friends. Secrets so big nobody would believe them without proof. Maybe the idea wasn't quite so out there after all.

CHAPTER FOUR

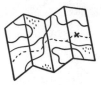

When we make it back to the campsite, Nate's kicked back reading a *Midnight Kingdom* comic, and Ezra's sitting on a stump scrolling through photos of him with his friends Jack and Zion. But instead of seeming happy, he looks totally bummed. Dad hustles past both of them and heads straight into the tent.

I scurry to Nate and whisper, "I need you to tell me everything that documentary said about the park ranger conspiracy."

Nate tilts his head. "I didn't think that sort of thing was up your alley."

I glance toward the tent. "I overheard Dad talking with Gramma about some kind of trouble in the park. And I found a silver tracker in his bag. Like the one we saw on the Komodo. I told him about our sighting at the river and I think he knows more but won't admit it."

"Whoa . . . this is just like what happened with a park

ranger in Yosemite. Only in that case it was a werecat she was hiding in her camper."

"Werecat?" I blow a strand of hair out of my eyes.

Nate nods gravely. "It was one vicious-looking kitty."

Before Nate can tell me any more about murderous felines, Dad emerges from the tent with his bag slung over his shoulder and a pair of walkie-talkies in his hands. He tosses one to me and clips the other on his belt.

"You're already leaving?" I know Dad's a grown-up and that he said he could handle the lizard on his own, but the thought of him facing off with the huge reptilian predator sets my stomach churning.

"You think you three can hold down the fort until Gramma gets back? You can buzz me if you need me." He gives me a knowing look and I nod.

Ezra glances up from his phone. "Sure. We'll be fine."

Dad mounts the yellow mare, and in a moment Daisy is trotting toward the river. A chipmunk stealing a mouthful of cheese puff has caught Nate's attention, and he's pulled out his camera to film. Meanwhile, Ezra's gone back to scrolling through photos and looking gloomy. Gramma and Dad said Ezra could bring a friend on the trip too, but he opted not to invite anyone. I figured he just didn't want to have to pick between his two besties. "You wish Jack and Zion were here?"

Ezra keeps his eyes on his phone. "Sorta . . . but it wouldn't really make a difference."

I peer down the trail after Dad and absently ask, "What do you mean?"

"Things aren't the same with Jack and Zion anymore. Or anybody. Stuff's different now."

I pull my gaze from the trail and study Ezra's face. His dark hair hangs over his eyes like he's trying to hide from the world. Ever since Ezra got infected, he's been quieter and when he does speak, it's usually about something strange—like the injured cockroach. "You just need more time. Things will get back to the way they were before."

Ezra stands and shrugs. "Maybe. Maybe not."

Before I can think of anything encouraging to say, Ezra starts for the hammock. I sit down on a log in front of the dying fire and open my journal. I thought this visit to Yellowstone would help bring everybody closer. Instead, things feel more scattered than ever. Dad's in some sort of trouble, and Ezra would rather stare at insects than hang out with me. I turn to a fresh page in my journal and reach for my box of colored pencils, then recall I left them on my sleeping bag in the tent.

I duck my head under the canvas door, grab my pencils. Dad's duffel bag catches my eye as I start for the door. I glance out the mosquito netting window. Dad and Gramma probably won't be back for at least another hour.

I don't like being sneaky, but I need info. I unzip Dad's bag and lift the small shiny band out. I slip it into my backpack and step out of the tent.

Nate waves. "Check this out, Mags!" He bends and lifts up a pair of twisted sticks. "Jackalope antlers!"

I give him a thumbs-up. "Nice."

I sit by the fire and slip the tracker out and fiddle with a dial on the back. A pair of chickadees tweets in the branches above. I add a few notes to my journal.

> Yellowstone Mystery
> Dad's in some kind of trouble
> Possible connection to Komodo dragon in park?
> Tracker found in his bag looks like tracker on lizard
> Conspiracy documentary about park rangers—
> fact or fiction?

I put my journal away and lift my head toward the trees. The birds have gone silent. Everything has. It's like every bug, bird, and animal in the park has suddenly frozen. Chills skate up my arms as a rumble moves through the earth. My legs rock, and my head whips side to side. It's like I'm riding the old wooden roller coaster at Thurby's Amusement Park and can't get off.

"The UFO invasion is upon us!" Nate screams, and zips around the yard like a maniac while miraculously still clutching his camera in one hand.

"It's not aliens." I wrap my arms around a tree trunk to keep from tumbling over. "It's an earthquake!"

The ground shakes and a groan fills the air. A pine tree creaks, then teeters forward. Branches snap and crack as the tree smashes down on our tent. Dust and bits of wood fling into the air.

Ezra grabs my arm. "We gotta get out of here!"

I sling my backpack over my shoulders, and the three of us bolt from the campsite. Dad said Yellowstone sometimes gets small earthquakes, but nothing about this feels small. The earth keeps rattling as we run into the forest. Pinecones rain down on us. I throw my hands over my head and squint to block debris from flying into my eyes.

"Maybe coming into a giant arsenal of tree bombs wasn't such a great idea," Nate says as he's pelted with a spray of acorns.

We pick up our pace and finally come to the clearing by the Firehole River. The water slaps against the shore in angry waves. The quaking seems to go on forever. I press my hands to the dirt, feeling queasy from all the shaking.

At last, things get calm again. Ezra turns our way. "You guys all right?"

I look myself over. I've got a scrape on the front of my leg, but nothing serious. "I'm okay."

"Whoa, check it out," Nate calls. He's leapt to a boulder at the edge of the river. In the distance, a blast of water as tall as a skyscraper rises above the tree line.

That's the direction Gramma went for the store run. I shudder, hoping she made it to town before it appeared. There aren't supposed to be any geysers that big around here.

"We definitely won't be going that way." Ezra jumps from one rock to the next, holding his phone up high. "I tried dialing 911, plus Dad's and Gramma's cells, but got nothing."

"Dad says cell calls hardly ever work in the backcountry. But we've got this." I lift the walkie-talkie off my belt loop and hit the talk button. "Dad, are you there?"

A stream of static follows, then Dad's voice breaks through. "Maggie? Is that you? Is everybody safe?"

"We're okay. Where are you?"

"I'm near Shoshone Meadows. I was following some tracks when the quake hit." Dad's voice is strained and followed by a low groan.

I frown. "You sound hurt."

"Daisy got scared when the quake started and threw me off. I don't think it's broken, but my leg's not in great shape. With the horse gone, it might take me a while to make my way to the campsite, but I'll do my best. When Gramma comes back, you can all head into town and wait for me there."

I survey the torrent of water spraying up in the distance. "Gramma can't get to us from town. There's a giant geyser in the way."

Another round of static follows before Dad replies. "Then hang tight in the tent. I'll get to you as quick as I can." There's rustling and Dad lets out another moan. From the sound of it, he's in no shape to be hiking all over the park to make it back to us.

I press down on the talk button again. "Our campground is smashed to bits. And you're hurt. We'll come to you. I've got a map in my bag. We'll be there soon."

"Maggie, Shoshone Meadows is four miles away from the campsite and with the quake—"

But before he can say more, the earth rumbles again. It's like a giant's going on a rampage and kicking everything in sight. A few basketball-size stones roll down and belly flop into the river with a splash. I jump back to dodge the spray, but as I do I lose my hold on the walkie-talkie. It crashes on the rocks and bounces into the shallow water at the river's edge. I scramble to fish it out, but the water is sloshing everywhere from the quake. When I finally get to it, it's soaked.

The ground rumbles, and more rocky grit skitters by. I

try to get Dad back on the walkie, but it's no use. Not even the sound of static comes out anymore.

I glance to Ezra and then Nate. "We're really on our own now."

"It won't be so bad," Nate says. "I've got fresh sneakers, and my camera's battery is fully charged." His eyes twitch to a pile of snapped-off tree limbs, and he gives a nervous laugh. "Imagine all the amazing footage we can snag for *The Conspiracy Squad* without any grown-ups holding us back."

Just then a boulder the size of a refrigerator tumbles toward us.

CHAPTER FIVE

We leap out of the boulder's path a split second before it smashes into the spot where we stood. It tumbles to the water making a splash that's taller than all of us. We turn and race away from the river. A cloud of dusty debris rises up. I cough and the air tastes like dirt. I can barely see as we sprint ahead. My lungs burn and my eyes sting when we finally come to a meadow fringed with reeds. We drop down in the tall grass and wait for the earthquake to pass.

When the rumblings stop at last, I look to Ezra and Nate. Their hair is coated with powdery dust, and their clothes are soaked and dirty. Nate pants and shakes his head. "Forget everything I said about grown-ups holding us back. No boulders ever tried to execute me when your dad was around."

"Hopefully, that was the last of the quakes." I open my backpack to take inventory of our supplies: a box of matches, bear spray, Gramma's homemade trail mix, a travel-size bottle of sunscreen, a flashlight, a half-empty canteen, the tracker, a map of the park, and my journal.

"Four miles of hiking out here isn't gonna be easy," Nate replies. "We've got earthquakes, a whole lotta stinky hot water poppin' up all over the place, plus a rogue Komodo dragon and whatever it is your dad's keeping secret. My guess is werewolves, by the way."

Ezra sits up straighter. "Hold up. Komodo dragon? Dad keeping a secret? That's all a joke, right?"

I bite my lip. "I was meaning to tell you, but things got a little wild back at the campsite. I know it sounds hard to believe, but Nate and I ran into a Komodo dragon at the river this afternoon. We don't know how it got here, but it had a tracking band around its foot, like somebody was keeping tabs on it."

"It was bloodthirsty, huge, and mega-fast," Nate adds in.

Ezra's jaw tightens. "And what about Dad having a secret? Is that true too?"

"I overheard him talking to Gramma. She was worried about him. I asked him about it on our hike, but he wouldn't tell me anything." I open my bag and pull out the silver band. "This was in his duffel. It's the same sort of thing that was on the Komodo dragon. It's got an antenna for tracking animals."

"And you think that means he had something to do

with a Komodo dragon being in the park?" Ezra asks, not looking convinced.

Nate nods. "I've done loads of research. Park rangers are basically a secret society hiding in plain sight. They're keeping more things under wraps than the Illuminati, Men in Black, and Area 51 combined."

I shrug. "Nate's been watching some documentaries that claim park rangers are in on a massive Bigfoot cover-up."

"Not just Bigfoot. Don't forget about the werecat in that lady's camper." Nate's eyes bounce from me to Ezra, seeming to pick up on the doubt in our faces. "It sounds wackadoodle, but you gotta admit something shady's going on with your dad."

Ezra stands and slides his hands into his pockets. "All we know so far is that Dad and Gramma talked about something they don't want you to know about and that he's keeping tabs on an animal. Which, given that he's a park ranger, is totally normal."

Nate grunts. "This must be how Finn Brody feels every day of his life."

"Finn Brody?" I ask.

"The documentarian," Nate answers. "He's always trying to convince people that cryptids like Bigfoot and jackalopes are real, but the world's jam-packed with doubters."

I blow a sweaty strand of hair out of my eyes. I can't

think about Bigfoot and jackalopes right now. "Let's just focus on finding Dad."

I pull out my map and locate Shoshone Meadows. "Even without horses, it should only take us about an hour and a half to reach him. The trail's east of us." I study the compass on my watch, then point to a shadowy bit of woods thick with soaring pines and dark gray mountains lurking beyond them. "Which is this way."

"You mean the way that seems even more out in the boonies than where we're at right now?" Nate asks.

"You said you wanted a chance to grab video for *The Conspiracy Squad*. Hiking the backcountry of Yellowstone will definitely give us some amazing footage," I answer.

Nate peers out over the woods and bounces on his toes, like he's psyching himself up. "If we're gonna take *The Conspiracy Squad* to the next level, we've gotta take some risks. No guts, no glory."

I glance up at the sky as the sun moves behind a cloud. Back home, going a few miles would be a breeze, but hiking here is a different story. I push down my nerves. The sooner we get going, the sooner it'll be over.

I tighten the straps on my backpack and we start for the woods. Nate pulls out his video camera, panning over steamy breaks in the dirt. "Deep in the heart of the earth, the insidious lava monster known as King Scorcho dwells. . . ."

I shake my head as we swish through the tall grass. Leave it to Nate to make the most out of any disaster.

As we walk, Ezra takes the lead, and Nate trails after me. Butterflies bob through the air, and birds sing, as if their whole world hadn't just been shaken out like a dusty rug. Maybe they can't help it. The park's filled with too much beauty and wildness for them to waste time being afraid. The sun's golden rays shine across the waving green grass. A clean, sweet smell rises up.

I reach out and pluck a tall blade and rub it between my fingers. I think about Dad. I really hope he didn't have anything to do with the Komodo running loose in Yellowstone. He once told me that there was a ten-thousand-dollar reward to catch the person who illegally introduced non-native lake trout into the park's waters. How much worse would things be for somebody who brought in a deadly predator? I break the blade of grass in two, then tear it again until it's nothing but green confetti.

"Hey, watch out!" Ezra grumbles as I bash into his shoulder. He's stopped walking and is staring at the meadow up ahead. The grass is all flattened down, like somebody took a jumbo-size rolling pin to it. There's a buzz and the familiar smell of sulfur.

"Are we getting close to another stinkpot?" Nate asks, curling up his nostrils.

I peer down at the map. "I don't think so. But then again, that giant geyser popped up after the quake, so I guess it's possible."

We take a few more steps. Flies waft into the air. There's dark fur in the grass. My muscles tense. Massive antlers stretch wide like a fallen chandelier. A hulking moose lies spread out on the ground. Claw marks crisscross its chest, and a pool of blood gathers beneath it. I've never seen anything this big dead before.

Nate shudders. "No earthquake took that thing down."

Ezra's face goes pale. He kneels next to the moose and gently nudges it with his hand. It doesn't move. He stands and peers around the meadow. "Why would an animal kill a moose and then just leave it here?"

Nate tilts his head toward the dark woods on the other side of the tall grass. "Unless whatever killed it is planning to come back later."

Something white and tissue-paper thin flutters near the moose's hooves. I kneel. It's easily six feet long, scaly, and delicate as a moth's wing. It's the shed skin of a reptile. A powerful one, capable of taking down a thousand-pound moose. "We need to get out of here. Now."

The grass behind us rustles. I slowly peek over my shoulder. A forked tongue swishes out of the tall brush. I scramble back.

The Komodo dragon juts forward, red-tinged drool spilling over its jaws.

"It's back!" Nate dodges away.

The lizard charges toward us, snapping at Nate's shoe. "You're not getting my sneaker!" Nate shrieks and dashes back.

Just then, a man with spiky, bleach-blond hair and a row of ear piercings sprints through the meadow. He's wearing a utility vest, khaki shorts, and black leather boots. He's a little younger than Dad and looks like a mix between a punk rocker and a zookeeper.

"No way! It's Finn Brody!" Nate hoots.

"The documentary guy?" I ask, but before Nate can answer two more people dart through the grass after Finn. One's a super-buff guy with an orangish spray tan and a black cat tattoo on his forearm. There's a video camera hoisted against his shoulder. An Asian woman with chin-length purple hair and headphones follows. She's holding what looks like a big fuzzy duster on a long pole.

The Komodo dragon locks eyes on the video camera and thrusts its tongue out.

"Unless you wanna be lizard food, you kids need to clear out," Finn calls, then spins toward the muscular man. "Check out that tongue. Can you get a close-up, Jake?"

"On it." The muscleman—Jake—positions himself between Nate and the Komodo dragon. "You're in the way of the shot, dude. Scram."

"How's the audio, Maki?" Finn asks the woman with purple hair.

Maki's stretched the duster-looking thing—which I now realize is a jumbo microphone—toward the Komodo dragon. "I can hear the flies buzzing and the daisies growing. We're good."

Nate spins toward me and stage-whispers, "We're on the set of a Finn Brody documentary! This is once-in-a-lifetime big."

I give a slight nod, wondering how much this film crew knows about handling large, aggressive predators. Nate pulls out his camera and alternates between panning over Finn and his crew and zooming in on the Komodo dragon.

Finn turns our way. He's got pasty skin that looks like he spends more time behind a computer than out in the field, and his eyes are such a bright blue that I'm pretty sure they have to be colored contact lenses. "You guys know who I am?"

Nate lowers the camera and beams at Finn. "I'm an ultra-mega-huge fan. I just binge-watched your whole series on cryptids hiding in our national parks. I wish more people knew about your work."

Finn cracks a smile. "You and me both. If you plan on posting that video later, make sure you tag me. There's no such thing as bad publicity. If you wanna be a filmmaker, always remember that."

The dragon lets out a low hiss, and we scramble back a few more feet. It gives us a final glare, then pounces on the moose. Its long, hooked claws slash at fur and bone. Ezra winces at the sounds of slurping and tearing.

Nate makes a gagging face and says, "This is even grosser than it eating the skunk."

"You guys have seen this thing before?" Finn asks.

"It chased us down at Firehole River this afternoon," I say. "But it shouldn't even be in the park. Komodo dragons aren't from around here."

"Native to Indonesia," Finn says as the lizard tears into another mouthful of moose. "We're out in the park this week trying to grab some Bigfoot video, but then the earthquake hit and next thing you know, Maki spots this dinosaur charging through the weeds. Figured we couldn't miss an opportunity to get it on film, even if it isn't a cryptid."

"Any luck catching Sasquatch on camera?" Nate asks.

Finn shakes his head, but there's a twinkle in his bright blue eyes. "Not yet. But we've been hearing chatter about some funky activity around the park. There's talk about a park ranger who's neck deep into something big. We're here to find out what it is."

Nate glances my way and I swallow hard. I don't think Dad's hiding Bigfoot or werecats, but he's definitely keeping something from us. Finn makes documentaries about park rangers with secrets. Even if Dad didn't mean any harm, Finn and his crew snooping around might spell trouble for Dad.

Maki lowers the microphone and looks our way. "I heard a radio broadcast saying the park's being evacuated. The earthquake was a 7.3 magnitude. Where are your parents? You three should be getting out of here."

"My dad went to check on some things before the quake. We're headed to him now." There's no way I'm telling these guys anything more about him.

Maki suddenly jumps back, the microphone pole tumbling from her hands. The Komodo dragon spins toward her and snaps its jaws around the mic's fuzzy top.

Jake jumps between Maki and the Komodo. It struts forward like a boxer stepping into the ring. Finn waves one arm at us. "Clear out. We'll handle it from here."

The Komodo's beady black eyes bounce to us. More red-tinged drool drips from its mouth. "If you ever need a backup cameraman, let me know!" Nate calls. "You can check out my work on—"

The lizard whips its armored tail and stalks our way. I yank Nate's arm and we bolt. As we run, the Komodo dragon picks up speed. Grass slaps against my legs as we race through the meadow. Ezra's in the lead, then Nate and me. Shouts join the sound of the lizard as it charges after us. The film crew is chasing after the Komodo. I pump my arms and run harder. Dark shadows fall over the grass as we near the thick evergreens up ahead. After a few minutes, the voices and swishing sounds fade. I peer over my shoulder. There's no sign of the lizard or Finn's crew, but we keep going anyway, not slowing down until we're deep in the woods.

When we've put enough distance between us and the Komodo, we finally stop to catch our breath. Nate and I drop down on the forest floor while Ezra paces around a cluster of bushes.

The last rays of sunlight sink behind the trees and there's a purple tint to the sky. I'm not even sure if we're headed in the right direction anymore. An owl hoots. Hiking in the daytime is one thing, but doing it at night is a much scarier can of worms. "I think we'd better make camp here for the night," I say.

"I was cool with roasting weenies and kicking back in the family tent, but this whole bunking down on some lumpy rocks with nothing good to eat? Not my style," Nate grumbles.

"No rock beds for us," Ezra answers, coming our way with a load of pine needles.

"What are those for?" Nate asks.

"Beds. A few years ago I read some book where the kids lived in the woods. They made beds out of pine needles and cooked stuff on an open fire. Everything turned out all right." Ezra drops a pile of needles, then gives them a little fluffing up.

I cock my head. "You're actually having a bit of fun with this, aren't you?"

Ezra smirks. "Maybe a bit."

Nate hums the *Jurassic Park* theme song under his breath while moonwalking around a birch tree. I guess he's not so miserable after all either.

"Let's see if the walkie-talkie has dried out," I say, and tug it from my belt loop. I click the switch and a light comes on. "It's working!" I hit the talk button. "Dad, are you there? It's me."

This time the staticky response comes out in broken spurts, and the light at the top of the walkie-talkie flicks off and on. "Can you hear me?" There's no answer. We're not going to make it to Dad tonight, and we don't have a way to tell him where we are. My shoulders tense, and there's a frustrated sting at the backs of my eyes.

All of a sudden static erupts from the walkie, followed by a familiar voice. "Magnolia Jane? Is that you, honey?"

Some of the tightness in my shoulders releases as I squeeze the talk button. "Gramma! Are you okay? Did you get hit by the geyser?"

"Nonsense. I was miles away by the time that thing blew. I told you all I was quick. And now they've got the whole park shut down and all the roads in closed off. But they've got rescue teams heading out to look for folks still stuck in the park. Now, let me talk to your daddy a minute and we'll get things figured out."

"We're actually not with Dad right now. He had to take care of something and we got separated before the quake."

"Are you telling me you're all alone in the wilderness with earthquakes and wolves and grizzly bears?"

"I'm not alone. I've got Nate and Ezra with me," I answer, glancing over at Ezra building up his pile of pine needles and Nate panning his camera over the woods. "We're doing fine. We're headed to Dad."

"Don't you go anywhere. Just tell me where you are right now, hon. Somebody's got to get you all out of there quick. The three of you tumble into danger like pigs to slop."

I crack a smile. "We're out in the woods near—"

The walkie chirps and the light on the top flickers. "Mag—" Her voice cuts out and the walkie-talkie goes dark.

"Gramma? Can you hear me?" I click the walkie off and on, but the light doesn't come back and neither does Gramma. I open the back where the batteries are. A yellow-orange crust has formed around the batteries. The water from the river is corroding them. I pop them out and tuck them in my bag to dry out and hopefully avoid any further damage.

I sigh and clip it back on my shorts. "At least we know Gramma's okay."

I sit down on a smooth rock and look over our make-shift campsite. We're stranded in the wilderness with plenty of dangers all around us. But surprisingly, I don't feel quite as awful as I'd expected. The first stars are blinking in the night sky, crickets chirp, and somewhere in the distance the river murmurs. There's not a hint of civilization anywhere near us. Backcountry Yellowstone is kinda scary, but it's also sorta exciting.

I glance at Nate and Ezra. If I have to be stuck out here, I'm glad I've got them by my side.

CHAPTER SIX

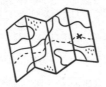

We get a fire going using some dried branches and a couple of matches. With the sun down, it's gotten a lot colder, making me wish I'd had time to grab a sweatshirt. We don't have any marshmallows or hot dogs to roast, but the flame's warm orange light makes the night feel calmer and less like something dark and hungry might creep out at any moment.

Ezra and I work to gather more sticks for the fire, while Nate stretches out on his pine needle bed, camcorder in hand.

"You know, you could help gather wood," I say, picking up a few small branches.

"I'm documenting our wilderness adventure. I want to be prepared in case we run back into Finn Brody. Who knows? He might want to join forces on his latest documentary. I've already got tons of stellar B-roll."

I dump the wood along the edge of the campfire. "We can't work with Finn. He makes documentaries about park rangers with secrets. Dad's a park ranger. We can't help Finn come up with any more material. Who knows what he might dream up about Yellowstone rangers?"

A knowing look dawns on his face. "Especially if he found out about a ranger who released a dragon in the park."

"We don't know that Dad had anything to do with that," Ezra chimes in.

"Even if he didn't, if Finn put it in a film, it would be bad for Dad."

"Finn's got a loyal following. The news would be all over the Internet," Nate agrees.

"Whatever we do, we need to stay as far away from Finn and his crew as possible," I say.

Ezra drops another pile of sticks near the fire. "Fine with me. I've had enough people with cameras asking questions to last me forever."

After Ezra got infected with the mutant fungus, the local news, and even a few bigger stations, all wanted to interview him about his experience. A few asked some pretty rude stuff—like whether he thought he'd lost brain cells from the experience or if he still felt human after being zombified for a week. I don't blame him for wanting to keep out of the spotlight.

Nate tucks his camera into his backpack and sits up. "So, what do we have in the way of munchies?"

I unzip my bag. "I've got trail mix, but I think we should save it for tomorrow. We've still got a decent amount of hiking to do before we'll make it to Dad. We ran about a mile from the river, but I'm not sure we went the right direction. So we could be even farther away than when we started."

"Here's my take. We eat the trail mix now and go full-scale caveman tomorrow," Nate suggests. "My stomach's already devouring itself. If I don't get some food soon, I'm gonna wake up with a giant hole in my gut."

"I've got a granola bar. You guys can split it," Ezra says, and breaks the bar in two.

"Aren't you hungry?" I ask, accepting one of the pieces.

Ezra sits down on his pile of pine needles. "I had one of those gross cans of little hot dogs while you guys were on the hike."

Nate stuffs his half in his mouth fast, before Ezra can have a chance to change his mind.

I munch on the granola bar and peer up at the sky. It's deep velvety black, with countless stars shining out like glittery pinpricks. I reach for the canteen and take a gulp. When I finish, I give it a shake. We'll have to start rationing our water. I lie flat on my newly made bed. It's not near as cushy as a real mattress or even my camp cot, but it's not terrible. The needles smell wintery and fresh, and if I position my hair just right I can keep them from poking into the back of my neck. The others have gotten quiet, and I wonder if they're already asleep. Ezra's arms lie folded across his stomach, and his chest rises and falls in a slow, steady pattern. In the distance, a wolf cry sweeps through the night.

Nate rustles on his pile of pine needles. "Did anybody happen to get a look at the moon tonight?"

"Huh?" I murmur.

"Do I have to spell it out? I'm talking werewolves."

Ezra rolls over, facing his back to the fire. "Get some sleep, man."

The wolves sound far away and probably aren't interested in us anyway. Back home, we hear coyotes, and strangely, the howls are almost comforting. "Everything will be all right." I yawn. The warmth of the fire spreads up my arms to my face, and my eyes slip shut.

The fire is out, and I'm shivering. Clouds black out the moon and stars. My pine needle bed is quaking, and I feel like somebody's picked up the ground under me and tossed it in the air.

"Ezra? Nate?" My hands bash against something sharp and rough, then I'm bouncing backward, rolling in a painful pile of arms and legs. The ground rumbles, and the air hisses.

My mind reels to what Dad said about Yellowstone quakes. That they sometimes come in swarms.

"Mags! I'm having that nightmare about being eaten by an overgrown hamster again!" Nate shouts.

In the distance, rocks crack together. Clouds of dirt explode around us. I duck my nose into my T-shirt. The rumblings and earth-splitting groans stretch on. More chalky dust spreads through the air, and I squeeze my eyes shut.

Just when it feels like the ground will never be still again, the rumbling finally slows, then stops. We flop back to the dirt and lie without speaking for a long time.

"Think it's done for good?" Nate asks at last.

I sit up. "I hope so."

"Let's see the damage," Ezra says, and reaches into his pocket. There's a scratchy sound, followed by a few sparks and a small flame. "I'll find a branch and get a torch going." There's more shuffling, and then the light brightens. He shines it over our campsite.

And I immediately wish he hadn't.

At the edge of what remains of our campsite, a large white wolf slinks over fallen rocks. Moonlight gleams down on its pale fur. It's beautiful in a dangerous, spine-chilling sort of way. The wolf tilts its muzzle toward the sky and howls. I hold my breath. A chorus of wolf cries follows. There's rustling in the brush, and one by one dark gray wolves close in.

I take a step back and bang into the wall of rocky debris behind us.

The white wolf releases another howl. It no longer sounds lonely or remotely familiar. The pack stalks closer.

They're apex predators and the only prey in sight is us.

CHAPTER SEVEN

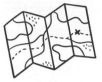

Ezra's torch flickers wild orange light over the pack. My heart pounds so hard it makes my head fuzzy. The wolves' musky scent floods the air as they close in. I can't think. I can barely breathe. The fur at the white wolf's neck bristles. If we don't do something soon, we're dead.

I grasp a branch and dip the end into Ezra's torch. It slowly ignites. As the light spreads, the blaze melts a tiny bit of the icy fear in my veins. For now, the wolves don't come any closer.

I glance toward the pile of rubble at our backs. It's too steep to climb quickly, and at least six wolves block the way through the forest. One wolf is bad enough, but in a pack, they can take down just about anything.

The white wolf's eyes are pale blue and its gums deep black. The others watch it closely. It takes another step. A bead of cold sweat runs down the back of my T-shirt. It has to be the alpha dog. The one that calls the shots for the rest of the pack. If we could scare it away, it might be enough to get rid of the others. If I knew where my back-pack was I'd try using the bear spray, but there's no time for searching for it now. "We've got to show them we're not afraid."

"But I *am* afraid," Nate says.

I clench my hand tight around the torch. "Then we've gotta fake it."

"How do we do that?" Nate whisper yells. "We don't have killer teeth or dagger claws or anything. What are we gonna do? A fight dance? A battle song? We're goners."

I bite my lip. Nate's being sarcastic, but it gives me an idea. If we can make enough noise, we just might be able to scare the wolves off. "Let's try it."

"Wait, what? We're seriously going to dance?" Ezra asks.

"Make noise. Take up as much space as possible. Let's show this pack we're nobody's dinner."

"If you say so, Mags." Nate pulls in a breath and spreads his arms wide. He belts out, "I will survive. . . ."

"Disco?" Ezra asks in disbelief as Nate sings out a loud, off-tune version of the old song.

"His mom does karaoke every Saturday night at Lumpy's Bar and Grill," I say as Nate shimmies and shakes his way across the dirt. "'I Will Survive' is one of her standards."

55

Two of the wolves throw their heads up, releasing their own high-pitched cries.

"It's working," I say, and join Nate for the third verse, adding in jazz hands to really sell it. Ezra pipes in too, and our voices pierce the night in a pitchy dance tune.

The white wolf's pale eyes shift from the three of us to its howling pack. It takes a few tentative steps back.

I smile. Nate's crooning just might keep us from being ripped to shreds.

We go for the grand finale, holding out the last note loud and long. Nate grabs Ezra's torch and tosses it into the air. It whirls up, the flame spinning like a comet spiraling just overhead. As it starts to come down, Nate attempts a move that can only spell disaster—a jump-kick-spin.

The torch flip-flops over itself twice, and just as Nate reaches out to grab it, it crashes to the dirt. A cloud of dust rises up as the flame goes out.

"That last bit looked a lot different in my head," Nate squeaks.

The alpha wolf growls. It seems to sense we're not quite as tough as we looked a minute ago. I wave my torch, but instead of blazing brighter, the flame shivers, then snuffs. We back up as much as we can until our bodies press into the rocky heap.

A wet snout brushes my calf. I kick my leg out and jaws snap at my shorts. I feel the wolf's hot breath on my skin as the fabric tears, and my knees go weak. I don't want to get devoured. Not by a pack of wolves or anything else. I suck in a huge breath and sing-shout, "We are the champions!" I raise my hands and give them a halfhearted wiggle.

Nate and Ezra join in the song, only this time our voices come out scared and shaky. There are too many wolves. We're not loud enough or strong enough to scare off one wolf, let alone a pack.

Yellow eyes reflect back at us in the darkness. Somewhere another geyser must be erupting; the air feels heavy and reeks of rotten eggs. My voice cracks. I can't sing any more songs about winning when I know we're about to lose big-time. There's a scrabbling sound, and the dim outline of something big and low to the ground. A chaotic stream of wolf howls follows.

"Ouch!" Nate hollers. "Something bit me!"

This is it. I wrap my arms around him, waiting for the wolves to finish us off.

"Sunny days sweeping the clouds away . . ." Nate barely whispers his twin brothers' favorite jam.

My eyes well up as I think about how much the maniacal three-year-olds will miss Nate if he doesn't make it back to Shady Pines.

A wolf whimpers, followed by barks and howls and a distinct hissing. It reminds me of when my tabby cat gets into nasty scuffles with the big, mean tomcat a couple trailers down from us.

I brace myself for the wolves to strike; the death blow. But instead of snarls and the pain from snapping jaws, their cries grow fainter. Then fade away altogether. The three of us stand in a huddle, our arms wrapped tight around one another. Bit by bit, the inky black sky shifts to gray, then amber.

I squeeze Nate and Ezra closer.

It's morning, and we're not dead.

CHAPTER EIGHT

Birdsong fills the air and I peer up. Rosy pink clouds smudge across a periwinkle sky. "Sunrise," I say. "I wasn't sure we'd get to see one of those again."

Ezra follows my gaze. There's a far-off look in his eyes, like he's taking in the pastel colors for the first time. Nate stretches his arms and yawns. Bright red puncture marks mar his forearm and rivulets of dried blood streak across his skin.

I reach for him. "That looks bad."

Nate rubs the spot. "It doesn't feel so great either, but at least the wolf decided Nate-chow wasn't on the menu and gave up after a nibble."

"Maybe that's what happened," I say, remembering the strange noises and the wolves growling. "Or maybe something scared them off."

"Either way, you need to clean it," Ezra says.

"Too bad we didn't grab a first-aid kit before the earthquake smashed up our stuff." Nate sighs.

I pull out my canteen. "For now, this is the best we can do." I pour a little water over the cut. When I'm finished, it looks just as bad, only wetter.

Ezra grimaces. "It's gonna get infected unless we find some alcohol wipes or something soon."

"On the upside, with a bite like this, I've got a pretty good shot of turning into a werewolf. Brigadier Ajax once got bit by a vampire beaver. It gave him the ability to digest wood, which came in pretty handy in the Forest of No Return," Nate quips, but his expression is more tired than playful.

"Maybe we can find some leaves to wrap it up in," I suggest.

"With our luck they'd probably end up being poison ivy," Nate says.

"We need to get out of the park. We're in way over our heads." Ezra pulls out his cell phone and raises it up over his head.

"Any luck?" I ask after a moment of Ezra pacing and holding his phone at a variety of angles.

Ezra shakes his head. "I sent Dad a couple of texts but they won't go through. Plus, my battery's down to seven percent. It'll probably be dead by lunchtime. How about the walkie-talkie?"

"We can try but the batteries looked pretty corroded last night. They might be ruined." Using the bottom of my

T-shirt, I wipe the crusty orange material off the batteries, then put them back in the walkie-talkie. I turn the power knob off and on a few times but nothing happens. "We won't be getting ahold of anybody on this for a while." I drop the walkie back in my bag.

"If we can't talk to Dad, we've got no way of knowing whether he'll still be at Shoshone Meadows by the time we get there. Maybe his leg healed up enough for him to start hiking. Or maybe he used his walkie to contact Gramma and have a rescue team get him out of there," Ezra says.

Ezra has a point. We have no real idea what's happening with him. But I can't see Dad leaving the park without coming to look for us first. "He knows we're headed his way. If a rescue team did get to him, he'd wait for us or send them out to find us."

"What if he runs into more trouble? Things don't seem to go as planned around here," Ezra says.

Last night's wolf attack is proof of that. I survey the campsite. Tufts of gray fur, blood, and a dark, sharp object I hadn't noticed before are scattered over the dirt. I take a few steps and kneel. It's a two-inch black claw. It's too long and thick to be a wolf's. I shift my eyes over the dirt. There are wolf tracks, but that's not all. A winding, ropelike pattern snakes between the hodgepodge of paw prints. Like something with a massive, swishing tail swept through the place. The Komodo.

I call over Nate and Ezra to update them on my theory.

"That would explain why the wolves cleared out so quick last night," Ezra says, picking up the claw and studying it.

I remember the eggy scent and the dark shape moving through the pack just before Nate got bit and the wolves cleared out.

I peer around the woods. The branches throw long, twisting shadows on the ground. Anything could be hiding out there, and we wouldn't know it until it was too late. "We should get going."

I glance at the compass on my watch, but sometime during the last earthquake, I must have cracked the glass. The screen's black, and when I hit the buttons, nothing happens. We're going to have to rely on trail markers to keep us on course today. Though after all the quakes, I'm not sure how many are still standing.

We slather on the last of my bottle of sunscreen and start off through the forest, munching the homemade trail mix as we go. The air smells damp and wild. Unseen creatures scuttle in the brush, and bugs buzz near my face. With each step my body gets sweatier and my throat drier. I give my canteen a shake. It's nearly empty.

It's been at least an hour with no sign of a real trail. We crawl over boulders and shuffle around brambles, all while trying to avoid getting roasted by steamy patches of earth.

None of us says much. I think we're all trying to save our energy knowing this could be another long day hiking.

At last, a swath of sunlight breaks through the trees. We scramble over a few more downed branches and come to a dusty trail at the edge of the woods. Only it's unmarked and forks in three directions. I pull the map out of my pocket, but I can't figure out which path we're supposed to take.

Nate rubs at his hurt arm. "We're lost, aren't we?"

I run my finger along the map, guessing at the location of where we stayed last night. "We're not exactly lost. Things just look different than I expected."

"That sounds a lot like lost to me," Nate says.

"Keep an eye out for any trail markers. Sometimes they get buried by brush," I say.

We walk on. Pink and blue wildflowers speckle the tall grass. In the distance, bison dip their humongous brown heads to munch on the blades. Farther out, gray mountains soar above it all. I inhale. Even the air smells like adventure. Yellowstone is wild and rugged and full of possibilities. It's true we've run into way more trouble than I ever expected, but we've also gotten to see a side of the park that most people never do.

"I think I found something," Ezra calls. He's standing by a clump of leafy green bushes.

"A trail sign?" I move his way.

"Lunch." Ezra holds up a handful of berries.

"Huckleberries!" I smile.

Nate eyes the dark blue berries suspiciously. "I thought eating mystery berries was a surefire way to end up stuck in an outhouse all day or worse."

"It is if you don't know what you're doing, but Dad pointed out the huckleberries to us when we got here, and these are definitely the same thing." I pop a few in my mouth and chew. Their sweet tartness spills over my tongue. Just a few swallows, and my throat already feels a little less parched.

"Here goes nothing." Nate pokes one berry in his mouth. He munches, looking thoughtful. "You know, it's actually not all that gross. I mean, it's not pizza roll good, but they're better than some of the boiled veggies my mom cooks."

"Check it out. There's something down here. It looks like an animal trap." Ezra kneels down at the bottom of the huckleberry bush.

Hunting isn't allowed in the park, but I can't remember if Dad ever mentioned researchers using traps to study animals. I edge forward trying to see what Ezra's found, but his back blocks my view. "I wouldn't touch that, Ezra. It might snap on you."

"I don't think so," he says. "It already caught something else." There's a metallic click, and then Ezra turns and faces me and Nate. He's holding a small, brown snake. It slithers and wraps itself around one of Ezra's wrists. Two bright yellow bumps the size of peas stand out on each of the snake's sides.

Nate backs away from Ezra. "Whoa, slow down there with that funky-looking viper."

"It looks like a rubber boa. I read about them in the Yellowstone guidebook on the car ride up. Only the ones in the book didn't have bumps," I say.

The snake writhes farther up Ezra's arm and Nate frowns. "There's no way that thing is rubber. It's moving."

"It got the name because its skin is sorta loose, which gives it a plasticky look. They're supposed to be some of the gentlest snakes around," I reply.

"But what's up with those growths?" Nate asks. "Do you think that's why someone was trying to catch it—because it's so gnarly looking?"

I bend down and examine the metal trap. It's tightly woven mesh and partially buried in leaves and forest debris. Inside, I spot two small springs with needle-tipped syringes attached. The tiny vials beneath the needles are empty.

Nate leans over my shoulder. "Do people usually inject their catches?"

"Maybe they were trying to give it medicine or put in one of those under-the-skin trackers," I answer. At the mention of trackers, my thoughts jump to the silver band I found in Dad's bag. Could this be a trap he set up? The needles' position lines up with where the snake's sides would be if it was still inside. Whatever was in those needles might be the cause of the snake's strange growths.

I carefully slide my hand into the metal box and detach the syringe from the spring. A glass vial is attached to the back of a thin needle.

"What is it?" Ezra asks.

I pull the vial close and read the tiny words written on a sticker along the side: *Cas9—NHEJ.* "Some kind of medical code, is my guess." I grab a crinkly napkin from the bottom of my bag, wrap the syringe up, and put it in the front pouch of my backpack so I can ask Dad about it later.

"Whoever was messing with this snake wasn't doing it any favors," Ezra replies. "He was probably just minding his own business when he got stuck in that trap and those needles shot into him. Now he's weird-looking and none of the other snakes are going to want to hang out with him anymore. He'll be stuck alone forever."

I don't bother telling Ezra that most snakes live alone anyway or that this snake might be a girl and not a boy. "Maybe it's only a little swelling from the medication. We're not sure what was in the vials. The puffiness might go back down soon and he'll feel like his old self."

"What if it doesn't?" Ezra snaps back. "He looks like a freak. Can you imagine how stressful this is for him, Maggie?"

Nate and I exchange a glance. Something about this snake has Ezra all bent out of shape. "I suppose sprouting lumps all of a sudden could be kind of hard for a snake," I say trying to sound as understanding as possible.

Ezra's jaw tenses. "I'm taking him with us. He needs somebody on his side."

I'm not so sure bringing a strange snake along is a great idea, but Ezra seems pretty determined and I've got bigger problems to worry about. Like the fact that I have no clue where we are.

I spread the map over the dirt. Growing up hiking with Dad, we got lost plenty of times, but he always managed to set us on the right path eventually. I try to think of what he'd tell me now.

I stand. If I can find the sun through the canopy, maybe I can figure out which way we're facing. I peer up, but it's no use. I can only see tiny snippets of sky between the branches. Not enough to give me any real sense of direction. I push my hands through my hair, then pause. It's the sound of water flowing nearby. I find a blue squiggly line on the map near where I hope we are. "That's got to be the Firehole River over there." I nod to the fork in the trail. "I know which way we should go."

Nate gives me a sideways look but doesn't argue. I wipe sweaty palms across the bottom of my T-shirt. The river might actually be a creek or a stream that's not even on the map. If I get this wrong, we could end up even more lost than we are now.

After a few minutes of hiking, the air gets stickier and the now-familiar stench of rotten eggs mingles with the smell of pine. The three of us come around a cluster of evergreens, and I scramble back. A stone's throw away, a geyser the width of a Jacuzzi tub shoots water twenty feet in the air. Mist sprays my cheeks. On one side of the blast, there's a thermal pool ringed in turquoise and sienna. Even without checking the map, I know I've taken a wrong turn. "That geyser's smack-dab in the middle of our trail. We're going to have to find another way."

"Pretty sure I know where we are," Nate offers.

"You do?"

"Remember that bird's nest by the fumarole we saw with your dad?" Nate points to a grassy heap near the edge of the geyser.

My shoulders fall. "We're back at the fumarole . . . only now it's a full-fledged geyser."

"And the eggs aren't just sitting around waiting to hatch anymore," Nate says.

Bits of crushed eggshells are sprinkled all over the mound.

I tilt my head. "But Dad said it was impossible. That the fumarole would roast anything that got close to it."

Nate shrugs. "In my experience, the impossible is way more possible than people give it credit for."

I eye the ground, noticing a pattern on the dirt. It's the same ropelike markings we saw between the wolf prints. They keep going all the way down to the nest. "I don't think those are sandhill crane eggs after all."

"I know." Nate nods to a leafy pile near the nest. At the top are his rope and flip-flop. The same stuff we lost in our first scuffle with the lizard. "Captain BiteyPants is a mama lizard."

"If even a couple of those lizards survive to adulthood, that'd be enough to cause a serious problem in the park." I peer around the thermal pool. "Most reptiles aren't protective parents, but just in case the Komodo comes back to check on her eggs, we'd better get away from the nest."

"Give me two secs, and I'll be ready." Nate scuttles toward the grassy heap, giving the geyser a wide berth.

"You can't get that close to the pool. You could get scalded!" I yell.

"I'm watching my step." He leans forward and plucks his flip-flop and rope from the nest, then jogs back my way.

Nate stuffs the sandal and lasso in his bag. I glance around, realizing Ezra's been silent this whole time. "Ezra? You ready?"

I wait a long moment, but there's no answer. I look to the trail. Softly swaying wildflowers and tall grass. And to the woods. Nothing but dark, shadowy branches. The only sound is the wind rustling through the leaves.

Nate meets my eye. "He's gone, isn't he?"

CHAPTER NINE

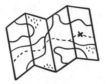

We spend at least an hour searching for Ezra, but there's no sign of him anywhere. My voice is hoarse from shouting his name, and an anxious knot has formed in my stomach. Worst-case scenarios run through my head. Ezra mauled by a grizzly. Buried in a landslide. Singed by a suddenly erupting geyser.

"Maybe the snake got loose and he chased after it?" Nate suggests.

"If he did, he could be anywhere by now." It wouldn't take too much walking to be completely and utterly lost in a place as huge as Yellowstone. And with the Komodo dragon and wolves on the prowl, staying in a group was our best bet for safety. I close my eyes and exhale. For now, we'll have to keep going and hope we bump into Ezra along the way.

After a while, we come around a bend. When the trail opens back up, I stop so fast I stumble over the toe of my sneaker. A white cloth flutters in the breeze. An old-timey prairie wagon stands in the middle of our path. There aren't any horses tied to it, but other than that, it looks exactly like something out of a history book.

"You thinking what I'm thinking?" Nate whispers.

I shake my head. "Probably not."

"We're time travelers, and we just walked through a massive portal."

"We're not time travelers."

Two little girls peek around from the wagon seat. They've got brown skin, dark curly hair, and matching pink sun visors.

"Hi." I wave.

They smile and giggle.

"Who's there?" A girl about my age with a braided ponytail and light brown skin comes from the front of the wagon. A pair of binoculars dangles from her neck. She's holding two plates loaded with fluffy golden triangles that look like fancy Toaster Strudels.

"You got breakfast pastries all the way out here?" Nate asks.

"It's not breakfast. It's today's special: pulled pork and potato pastry pockets." She hands the plates to the other two girls and glances back at Nate, who hasn't taken his eyes off the food. "Are you robbers? Cause if you are, I'll have you know I'm a white belt in karate."

Nate cocks his head. "Don't kids start out as white belts?"

"Doesn't matter." She plops her hands on her hips.

"We're not robbers. We're paranormal investigators," Nate says.

"Only in our spare time," I add. "I'm Maggie, and this is Nate. Our campsite got crushed in the quake, and now we're looking for my brother and dad."

"You guys are weird but you don't seem dangerous," she says, then relaxes her arms. "I'm Penelope. And these are my little sisters, Samantha and Tully."

"We're not little," one of the girls answers. She's the taller of the younger sisters and is missing both her front teeth. "I'm five and a half and Tully's almost four."

Penelope rolls her eyes. "All right, fine, you're big girls. Now, do you want to meet some new people or not?"

At that, the younger girls leap from the wagon seat and dash our way. The smaller one, who's sporting yellow rain-boots and a row of glittery stickers down one arm, wraps her arms tight around Penelope's leg.

"I know that move," Nate says. "My little brothers are always getting me in the death grip. Impossible to break out of without falling on your face."

"You just gotta know the right way to handle the situa-tion." Penelope stiffens her body and raises her chin. "Let go this instant, Tully. Or you're gonna be sorry."

Tully sighs and breaks her hold on Penelope's overalls.

Penelope gives Nate a quick that's-how-it's-done look and then turns back to me. "So, is your missing brother a skinny teenager who talks to animals?"

I bounce on my toes. "You've seen him!"

Penelope laughs. "Now I know for sure you guys are weirdos. We saw him an hour ago. Said he was helping a snake."

Definitely Ezra. "Did you see which way he went?"

She motions to the path on the other side of the wagon. "Down the trail to the left."

I peer at the map. That's the way to Shoshone Meadows, where Dad is. It sounds like Ezra is at least headed in the right direction. "Thank you!" I spin to Nate. "Let's get going. Maybe we can catch up with him and still make it to Dad before dark."

But Nate's eyes are now locked on a sign nailed to the side of the covered wagon.

"Pop's Prairie Pantry," Penelope says, following his gaze. "Up until yesterday we were running the best chuckwagon in all of Yellowstone. We traveled around the park serving up our culinary goodness on wheels. But then our Clydesdale, Giddy-up, ran off. My parents left me in charge while they went to find him. Of course, that was before the first earthquake struck and they closed the park." The grass rustles and Penelope's eyes dart to the dark shadows just behind the meadow. She lifts the binoculars to her eyes. When she lowers them, she lets out a shaky sigh. "Just a bluebird."

"Have you heard from your parents since the quake?" I ask.

Penelope glances at her sisters. "Not just yet."

I give a reassuring smile to Samantha and Tully, who peer up at me with big, worried eyes. "I'm sure they'll be back in no time," I say, and turn Nate's way. "We'd better get moving if we're going to catch up with Ezra."

"You're leaving? Just like that? Don't you want to stick around and have some lunch?" Penelope asks, her voice tilting a little higher and louder than before.

Nate glances at the wagon. "I could definitely go for some chow that isn't nuts and raisins or mystery berries."

The thought of home-cooked food sets my mouth watering. I crane my neck and take a peek inside the wagon. The shelves are lined with cans of food, jars of colorful pastel taffies, and old-fashioned toys like slingshots and yo-yos. There's a hot plate plugged into a boxy generator and a pitcher of ice tea sitting on top of a big red ice chest.

"Maybe we could spare a few minutes if you're sure you don't mind sharing," I say.

"We've got plenty," Penelope says. "Sit tight. I'll have it out in a sec."

A few minutes later, she comes back with plates heaped with the most beautiful golden pastry puffs on the planet. Samantha and Tully trail her with red plastic cups filled with ice tea.

They spread a paisley blanket on the grass, and Nate and I drop down and start shoveling the savory pastries into our mouths. After a few bites Nate sighs like he's in paradise. "This is literally the best food that has made contact with my taste buds in the history of ever." A bit of pulled pork hangs on Nate's chin.

"Told you they'd like it," Tully says, jabbing Samantha in the ribs with her finger.

"I was the one who told you," Samantha argues.

"Was not."

"Was too."

Penelope shakes her head and sighs like she's fresh out of tricks for wrangling younger siblings.

I take a bite of the cherry pie pastry. It's got a sweet cinnamon flavor at first, followed by a little kick that makes the sides of my mouth tingle. I lick my lips.

"Good, right?" Penelope asks with a sideways grin.

"Very."

As Nate and I chew, Penelope lifts the binoculars again and peers out toward the shadowy woods. She keeps them pressed to her face for a full minute while she homes in on an especially dark bit of the forest.

"Another bluebird?" I ask.

"Could be," Penelope says, then turns to her sisters with a smile that looks a little too big to be real. "How about you girls help me clean up a bit? If you get the kitchen all nice and tidy, I'll play freeze tag with you later."

"Are you gonna say stuff you don't want us to hear?" Tully asks, pushing the toe of her rainboot into the dirt.

Penelope drops the smile and crosses her arms. "Just help me out, all right?"

Samantha and Tully hop up and take a couple of empty plates into the wagon. When they're out of earshot, Penelope leans in close. "I don't know how far you guys are planning to hike, but I'd be careful out there. Things have been a little strange around the park lately."

"What do you mean by 'strange'?" I ask.

"I like bird-watching," Penelope answers, touching the tips of her fingers to the binoculars. "Chickadees, swallows, flycatchers, kingbirds . . . they've all been off lately. They're abandoning nests, making distress calls, and eating food they'd usually leave alone."

"What do you think would cause something like that?" I ask, scooting in a little closer.

"I've been tracking the behavior of each species," Penelope says. She reaches for a colorful notebook on the seat of the wagon, then sits down next to us and opens it to a page with handwritten graphs full of data.

"This is amazing," I say, scanning lines of information detailing shifts in behavior for each species.

Nate swallows a big bite of pastry. "Fascinating stuff. Mind if I eat the last popover?"

Penelope pushes the plate toward him. "Have at it."

"At first, I thought all the weird stuff could have something to do with the weather. But I've accounted for that here." Penelope points to another graph on her page. "The birds' behavior doesn't match up with any temperature shifts or storm pattern that I can figure. So, I've got a different hypothesis."

"What is it?" I meet her eye.

Penelope arches one brow dramatically. "I think a new predator might be moving into Yellowstone. Something these birds haven't seen before."

At that, Nate's head whips up from his plate of food. "What kind of predator are we talking about? Big, hairy, walks on two legs, leaves mondo-size footprints wherever he goes?"

Penelope purses her lips. "You mean Bigfoot?"

"The park is a known hot spot for the big guy. I'm just saying Sasquatch could be the reason the birds are acting funky," Nate says.

"Or maybe something huge and reptilian," I say, reminding Nate that there's a much more likely explanation, but he just stares at me like my words aren't getting through. Bigfoot can have that effect on him. I sigh and add, "Maybe something in the *dragon* family."

"You guys believe in dragons and Bigfoot?" Penelope slowly closes her notebook.

Before I can explain that the dragon I'm talking about isn't mythical, Nate chimes in. "Mags and I are cocreators of what's probably gonna be the next big Internet sensation. We've got a whole show dedicated to the weird and unexplained. Aliens, werewolves, Bigfoot, the works. You may have heard of it, *The Conspiracy Squad*?"

"Afraid not," Penelope says, looking less interested by the second.

Heat rises to my cheeks. When Nate lays it all out there, we do sound kinda nutty.

"Well, be on the lookout. Our stars are on the rise," he adds.

Penelope peers from me to Nate with a flat expression. I'm pretty sure she's not going to be checking out our channel anytime soon. "Nate, can you show Penelope the video you got out in the meadow? I think it might help clear things up."

"Always happy to share our work," Nate says, and retrieves his camera from his bag. Within seconds, he's found the video with the dead moose and the Komodo dragon.

As Penelope watches, her face shifts from skepticism to

fear. When it finally ends, she's silent for a long moment. Samantha thrusts her head out from the wagon. "Can we come out now? We want to watch TV too!"

"No!" Penelope snaps, then pulls in a breath and smooths her braid. "Give me five more minutes and I'll throw in a round of bedtime tickles."

"But not on my feet! That's too tickly!" Samantha grins and pokes her tongue between the gap in her front teeth.

"So there's a Komodo dragon on the loose in Yellowstone." Penelope's brows tug together. "Any idea how it got here?"

I twist a strand of hair around my finger tight, hoping Nate won't mention anything about Dad or Finn Brody's theory on rangers hiding creatures in the park. "We're still trying to figure that out."

Penelope rewinds the video and watches it again. "That lizard is big . . . but I don't think it's enough to explain all the changes I've been seeing."

"You don't?" I ask.

"With the family business, we travel around here quite a bit. The changes I've seen are happening in too many places for one Komodo dragon to be responsible for it all."

Nate nods knowingly. "I knew it. It's Bigfoot."

Penelope sighs. "You're really into Sasquatch, aren't you?"

I peer out over the meadow that stretches toward the

edge of the woods. In the distance, mule deer graze on the tall grass, and purple lupine flowers sway in the breeze. If Penelope's right, there's a new threat moving into the park. And it may be even more dangerous than our Komodo dragon. I think of the conversation I overheard with Dad and Gramma. How she worried that he was into something that might get him hurt. The longer we stay here, the longer Dad and Ezra are on their own, getting into who knows what kind of trouble.

I stand and dust off my shorts. "It's late. We really should get going now."

"You sure you don't want to stay the night?" Penelope asks, hopping up after me. "We have plenty of food and blankets."

The thought of eating pastries with Penelope and her sisters, camping out around the wagon, and waiting for help to show up is tempting. But Ezra's missing and Dad's hurt. I can't quit until we're together again. "Thanks for the offer, but my family is still out there."

"I get it. Family first." She nods, but still looks nervous. Things are rough for me and Nate, but Penelope's in a tight spot too. Plus, she has her little sisters to worry about.

"Thanks for the food. It was amazing." I open my bag and pull out my can of bear spray. "Here, take this. Just in case."

Penelope shakes her head. "You don't need to give me anything."

"It's a thank-you for lunch." I glance to the woods. "Besides, it might come in handy."

She looks at the bear spray for a moment, then nods and takes it. "Thank you."

Nate stands and gives a low groan. A pink flush creeps along his arm. I bite my lip. It looks like an infection. "You wouldn't happen to have a first-aid kit around here, would you?"

"Let me see what I can find." Penelope disappears into the wagon. A moment later she returns with a handful of Disney Princess Band-Aids and a small bottle of hand sanitizer. "Sorry it's not more."

"This is great," I say.

Nate grimaces but pops the lid open and squirts a quarter-size blob around the bite on his arm. His face contorts and he howls. We get his arm bandaged, and then I turn back to Penelope. "I guess we'd better get going. Thanks again for everything."

"Good luck." Penelope wraps an arm around each of her sisters. "I hope you find your family soon."

"You too," I reply, and we set off into the wilds alone again.

CHAPTER TEN

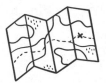

With our bellies full, Nate and I seem to cover more ground faster, at least at first. Every few feet there's either a boulder in our path, a steaming crack in the earth, or a fallen tree. We call for Ezra at each new turn, but so far, no luck.

The longer we walk, the more Nate drags. We've barely slept in the last twenty-four hours, and neither of us is used to so much hiking in rough terrain. On top of that, Nate's looking feverish. Possibly from the wolf bite.

"Need a break?" I ask. "I'll find you some more huckleberries. That might put a little pep in your step."

"I'm not hungry. I just need to sit a sec." Nate sinks to the dirt and drops his head between his knees.

I slide down by his side. As we rest, the sun slowly descends in the sky. Part of me wishes I could stuff my head between my knees too and just wait for somebody to come and find us. Preferably somebody with a large lemonade and a grilled cheese sandwich. But that's not going to happen. Nobody knows where we are. And even if they did, with all the earthquakes and landslides, Yellowstone is in chaos right now. Dozens of tourists are probably stranded in the park. We're going to have to fend for ourselves for a while longer.

Even after applying the alcohol, Nate's got puffy streaks running down his arm. I jab a stick into the dirt while I try to come up with options. But I can't think of any quick fixes. All I know is that I don't want to spend another night out in the open.

I pull out the map. From what I can tell, we're only about two miles from Shoshone Meadows. If we hike fast, we could be there by dark. I look Nate over. His head is still between his legs, and he's gotten so quiet I wonder if he's fallen asleep. "You sure you don't want me to grab you some berries? You could keep resting while I look."

Nate lifts his head, giving his curls a shake. "Ezra's already vanished, and for all we know he's been abducted by aliens or kidnapped by Sasquatch. I'm not letting you out of my sight."

Dark half-moons rest beneath Nate's eyes, and his cheeks are pink with sunburn. If he feels as bad as he looks, he's gonna need more than a second before he's up to hiking again. Maybe if he drifts off for a bit, I can slip away for a few minutes to look for berries. My focus shifts to some bushes not too far away.

Nate grits his teeth. "Seriously, Mags. No solo adventures. We stick together, okay?"

"Fine, but we need to get moving soon, or we'll be camping out alone again."

"Almost ready." He gives a faint smile and stretches his legs out toward the grass. His eyes slide shut and after a while, his breathing falls into the heavy pattern of sleep. As he dozes, the forest grows darker. An owl hoots from the treetops, and a shiver runs down my spine. I don't want to think about what else might be lurking nearby. I unzip my backpack and take out my journal to update it with the most recent events.

Komodo dragon takes down 1,000 pound moose
Finn Brody film crew in park—on the hunt for
a conspiracy
Animal trap set with mysterious needles
Birds acting strange throughout Yellowstone

Finn Brody said there'd been a lot of chatter about the park lately. Penelope's noticed oddities too. That combined with what we've seen ourselves, plus whatever Dad's keeping secret, all equal a big mystery. There's got to be some kind of connection, but I can't figure out what it is yet. I close the journal. As the forest grows darker, my legs itch to get on the trail. Anything would be better than sitting here waiting for something bad to happen, but I promised Nate I wouldn't leave his side.

I focus on the dim prairie beyond, searching for any signs of movement. After a while, all my worries fall away under the weight of my eyelids. Scenes of Ezra and the snake, exploding geysers, and a slinking Komodo dragon slip in and out of my dreams.

"You gonna keep snoring forever, or can we get this show on the road?"

My eyes snap open. Nate stands over me, sporting a sideways grin. "Told ya all I needed was a sec."

I blink. The sky's a dingy gray, and the temperature's dropped at least ten degrees. "Think it's safe to hike this late?"

"It's either that or we hang out and wait for the werewolf gang to make a repeat visit."

I take a look around the woods. The sun's already set, but there's still enough light to walk for a little while. We can't make it to Shoshone Meadows before nightfall, and I really don't want to make pine needle beds and sleep under the stars again. Not when there are so many unknowns in the park. I examine the map, searching for any shortcuts. Instead, I notice a small black square not far from where we're at. There's a note at the bottom of the map that corresponds to the square: U.S. ARMY CORPS OF ENGINEERS CABIN, BUILT 1905, *NO LONGER IN USE.

I read about these cabins in the guidebook. "I think I found a place for us to stay tonight. A long time ago, the army built a bunch of backwoods cabins in Yellowstone. There's one not far from here."

"Any chance it includes a hot tub and a free continental breakfast?" Nate asks.

"It's probably just a dusty old shack, but at least it'd give us some shelter."

Nate smiles feebly. "Ah well, beggars can't be choosers."

We hike in silence. My feet ache, and my throat's so dry it feels like I swallowed a cactus. After the massive lunch with Penelope, I thought I'd never be hungry or thirsty again. But hiking burns food like nobody's business. My canteen's empty and my stomach rumbles.

Nate keeps by my side until the trail narrows and we have to walk single file. After a while, his footsteps fall behind. I stop and turn around. He's leaning against a tree.

"How you doing? Wanna stop for a minute?" I ask, even though the thought of sitting down again brings a panicky flutter to my chest.

Nate looks up at the sky. "Getting darker."

"Yeah." We've been saving the batteries in the last flashlight, but now seems like as good a time as any to use it. I click it on, and a thin yellow beam shines out.

We crunch past sagebrush and pinecones. Finally, we come to a faded sign. There aren't any words, just a symbol of a square with an upside-down V on top. "I think this is it. The marker for the old cabin. Less than a fourth of a mile away," I say trying to sound perky, but my eyes drift to the path ahead. It's overgrown with brambles and weeds, like nobody's come this way in years.

Nate peers down the trail. "Do you think we made the wrong choice?"

"You mean trying to find this cabin?"

"I mean all of it. Leaving the first campground. Searching for your dad. Trying to get epic videos for *The Conspiracy Squad*."

I rub one hand over the back of my neck. It's damp with sweat that's gone cold since the sun went down. The moonlight casts silvery shadows on the tangled path ahead. It's too late to start over, but if I had the chance, I'd take a redo. Beginning with letting Dad go off without us. Then later, when that first earthquake hit and our campsite got crushed, hiking to Dad felt like the smart choice. But now I'm not so sure. If we'd stayed close, a rescue team might have found us eventually. And we probably wouldn't have lost Ezra either.

"We may have made a few mistakes," I admit.

CHAPTER ELEVEN

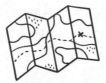

Coyotes howl in the distance, followed by the low, mournful hoot of an owl. Bony branches scrape against our arms, and brambles tug at our feet. If hiking the main trail was hard, this is nearly impossible. The flashlight's beam flickers, and I whisper a prayer that the batteries hold out until we find the cabin.

I push my legs faster. We weave around piles of rubble. There's an opening in the thicket, and for a moment we hike without worrying about being thrashed by thorny branches. I scan the wilderness for any sign of a man-made building, but there's nothing.

As my hopes sink, so does my foot—dropping down hard into a low spot in the dirt. I stumble, and a stabbing pain shoots up my ankle. Nate thrusts out his arm. I grab it like it's a life preserver saving me from stormy waters, but when I try to stand, my leg gives way under me.

"You okay, Mags?"

I touch my fingers to my leg, then wince. "I think I twisted my ankle."

"The cabin can't be much farther, right?" Nate slides my arm up and over his own and wraps it around his shoulder. We get going again, but our movements are slow and awkward. With every step there are fallen branches, prickly brambles, and pinecone tripping hazards. It's like nature itself booby-trapped the place.

As we press on, I start to worry that there is no cabin. What if the mark on the trail is only showing where the building used to be a hundred years ago? With my ankle and Nate's infected bite, our pace is snaillike. At last, I stop and shake my head. "It's not here. We need to turn around."

Nate shines the flashlight over the woods. There's only vines and grass and tree branches. He nods, and we slowly start back. Without the hope of shelter to spur us on, the hike out of the woods feels even harder. After limping a few more steps, Nate says, "How about we rest a minute?"

I'm too tired to argue. We stagger toward a leaf pile. When we make it there, I notice it's more like a leaf tower than a heap. It's taller than us by a few feet and stretches as wide as Gramma's carport back home.

Nate peers up at it. "It looks like every leaf in the forest comes here to die."

"At least it'll be nice and fluffy. Like a giant bean bag

chair." I drop down and start to lean into it, but instead of smooshing in, my back hits something solid.

I run my hand across the hard surface. As I do, my fingers catch on what feels like a rope hammock. "I don't think this is a leaf mountain after all."

I grab hold and tug. The leaves suddenly slide away and drop to the forest floor. In their place is a rustic wood building.

"Whoa, stealth mode unlocked," Nate breathes. "It's like what my dad uses to cover stuff up when he goes out dove hunting with my uncle Tony. But why hide some junky old cabin out in the middle of nowhere?"

I study the faded wooden sides and sagging roof. There are a couple windows, a stone chimney, and a front door. "Maybe the camo's to keep people like us out. But this is an emergency situation. We're not just some nosy tourists."

Nate feels around for the doorknob with a frown. "Too bad dumps like this are always loaded with my archnemesis, the arachnid."

He pushes the door open, and we tumble inside. A smoky smell rushes into my nostrils. It's instantly warmer, and there's a faint hum coming from somewhere nearby. I slide my back against the wall. Pain pulses through my leg, and I close my eyes.

"Hey, Mags?"

"Yeah?" I crack one eye open. A red light blinks in the far-left corner of the dark room.

"Do hundred-year-old abandoned cabins usually have surveillance cameras?"

CHAPTER TWELVE

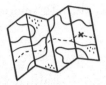

shine my flashlight toward Nate. He pats around the walls till he finds what he's looking for. Light spills over us.

"Whoa," we both murmur.

This place isn't deserted. It's outfitted like something out of a spy movie. TV screens showing night-vision images of the woods, metallic gadgets I don't recognize, and a wall decked out with marked-up maps of the park.

Nate moves around the cabin in a slow circle. "The way I see it, we're looking at two possibilities. One, this place is the lair of some evil nature villains or two . . ." Nate gives a long pause, surveying the room again. "Nah, that's pretty much the only option."

"A villain lair?" I ask, turning toward a rustling sound coming from the cabinet next to me. The shelf's loaded with glass jars housing strange scurrying creatures.

"If there's a spider anywhere up in that mess, then these people are certified grade-A monsters. End of story. Nobody but villains keeps spiders for pets."

I scan the jars. There are dozens of them, each with a paper label stuck on the side.

"Think this might have something to do with the snake trap or the funky bird stuff Penelope was talking about?" Nate asks.

I wish I could say that I didn't think there was any connection. But finding a hidden lab filled with creepy crawlers sure seems to point to some kind of unauthorized research project. And I can't help worrying that Dad might be involved. All I can hope is that there's a reasonable explanation for what we're seeing. I scoot closer to the cabinet, but as I move, pain zings down my foot, and I have to stop a second to catch my breath.

"You okay?"

"Just a little sore." I grit my teeth and pick up a petri dish. The water inside the dish is ringed with the same colors as the thermal pools in Yellowstone. I read the label along the side. *Sulfolobus acidocaldarius; thermophilic extremophile produces sulfuric acid. Ideal temp 158–176 Fahrenheit; Optimum pH 2–3*

"You understand any of that?" Nate peers over my shoulder.

I read the label again. "*Thermophilic* means 'heat-loving.' I watched a show once called *Earth's Extremophiles and Where to Find Them*. It was all about creatures that can survive outrageous conditions. Burning hot, freezing cold, acidic, super salty. They thrive where most other species would die."

"Sounds a lot like the shapeshifting cyborgs Brigadier Ajax visited on his way to the intergalactic council in issue 107." Nate taps his chin. "But they ended up being no good dirty rotten thieves who stole his teleporter."

"Well, I don't think we have to worry about the thermophiles robbing us. They're microscopic." I set the petri dish down and pick up a jar filled with liquid. A squirmy red-and-white worm flits up and down. The label reads *Thermal Vent Worm*. Under the name, there's some sort of coding. *TGH-.003; HTC .00047%; size 10X*. I give the wriggling creature a closer look. It has no eyes as far as I can tell, but rows of needle-sharp teeth. I hold out the jar to Nate. "Check it out."

"Dang, that's one seriously ugly worm."

"Maybe you'd better grab some video. I'm pretty sure 'Maggie's Minute' fans are gonna want to see this," I say, wondering if Nate's not feeling so well again. Normally, he'd hop to filming without me ever having to ask.

Nate gives the worm a skeptical look but fishes out his camera anyway and pans over the shelves. "It's grody, but grody gets views. After I add some spooky background music, this whole segment is gonna be spook-tastic."

I set the jar down and reach for another. This place is creepy but also sort of amazing. There's loads of gear and specimens and everything I wish our science lab back at Shady Pines Middle School had for us to research. I examine a creature scuttling side to side in its glass jar. This one I recognize without even reading the label. A desert scorpion. It's a big one too. Pale yellow with two fierce-looking pincers and a curled-back tail ready to strike. There's more indecipherable coding along the side of the jar as well. "Get a close-up of this guy. His claws are really something."

"Is that what I think it is?" Nate cringes. "You told me last summer scorpions are arachnids."

"That's right." I sigh, knowing where this is going.

"And spiders are arachnids."

"It's in a jar, Nate. It's not going to sting you."

Nate gives his head an offended shake. "That's not the point. That thing is basically an armored spider with a tail full of pain. That does it. Whoever's camped out here needs to be locked up right away."

"It's not a crime to study arachnids, Nate."

"I beg to differ."

I set the scorpion jar down and scan the remaining containers. Small blue fish swish in a few. There's a petri dish with a colorful swirl spreading across the bottom. The last couple of jars appear to be filled with nothing but water. But when I squint, I realize something translucent is swimming around inside. "Fascinating," I murmur.

"Nope, not fascinating. I don't care what you say, people who convert rickety old cabins into warehouses for the nastiest critters on the planet are foul."

I bite my lip, wondering whether it's crossed Nate's mind that Dad might have something to do with this place. Because the more I look around, the more this cabin seems like it's filled with all the sorts of things that most captivate Dad. "Remember what you told me about Finn Brody and his theory about park rangers keeping things like Bigfoot a secret? Does he ever say why they do it?"

Nate lowers the video camera and scratches his chin. "Not exactly, but he did interviews with some of their family members. A lot of them said they thought it was because the rangers didn't get enough recognition. It ticked them off that people took them for granted, so when they had a shot to be a part of something super top secret, they jumped on it."

After Dad got fired last year, things were pretty rough for him. Nobody in town took him seriously as a scientist anymore. He couldn't find work and, in the end, he had to move a thousand miles away.

Nate slowly blinks. "You're not thinking this place might belong to your dad, are you?"

I raise one shoulder, then let it fall. "I don't know what I should think right now."

Nate peers around the room like he's seeing it with brand-new eyes. "When I said this may be a villain's lair, I was just joking. Even if this place is his, that doesn't make him a bad guy. Maybe he just wanted to set up a little side project."

"What about the rogue Komodo dragon? And the snake injections? And the birds leaving their homes? There's gotta be a connection and Dad might be it."

"I know I'm usually the one jumping to conclusions, but this time I think we need to slow down a bit. We don't know that your dad has anything to do with this cabin or any of the rest of it. Let's just wait until we can talk to him."

I press my fingers against my temples. Nate's right. Making assumptions won't help anything. "Okay," I agree. "And thanks."

"For what?" Nate asks.

"For not believing the worst about Dad."

Nate grins. "Anytime."

I slowly rise to my feet and peek around the cabin. There's a small kitchen in one corner and another space in the back where I can just make out bunk beds pushed against the wall. "At least we can restock our supplies and sleep here for the night. We can look for Ezra in the morning."

I hobble to the kitchen and dip my face under the faucet. I guzzle down cool water until my belly's sloshing with liquid. It feels good to not be crackling from the inside out. I fill my canteen from the sink and then open the mini-fridge. I smile. It's fully stocked. I drop a few water bottles, three oranges, and a bag of grapes into my backpack. Under normal circumstances, I'd feel rude rummaging through a stranger's fridge and taking their food without permission, but this is a survival situation. Following the normal rules won't keep us alive.

Nate whoops. "I found two bags of Flamin' Hot Cheezy Poppers in the cabinet." He rips open a bag and shoves a few crunchy orange puffs into his mouth. "Plus, I spotted a bottle of Tylenol in there. I figure it'd be good for your ankle. That, and my werewolf bite is getting kinda sore again."

"You'd better wash that thing off with some soap and water while we're here."

"Yeah, sure," Nate says. "It's getting a funky crust on it anyhow."

"Ew. Let me see."

Nate pulls back a couple of the Band-Aids and holds out his arm for my inspection. The puncture marks on his forearm are red and puffy. I touch the skin around the bite. It's hot. "It's infected for sure. We'd better look around for some antibiotic cream." I eye a cluster of beakers and a fancy-looking microscope. "Just be careful. A lot of this stuff looks really expensive."

"You can call me Mr. Silky Paws." Nate wriggles his fingers in a way that assures me we're not getting out of here without at least a few shattered bottles.

I open more drawers and find an extra-long dish towel. There's no freezer on the mini-fridge, so I can't ice my leg. Instead I run the towel under cold water, wring it out, then wrap my ankle tight. I hold the makeshift bandage in place with the couple of hair bands I keep around my wrist for emergency ponytails.

I shuffle around the room, looking for a phone or a laptop, but in spite of all the tech, there's no sign of any communication devices. I sit on the windowsill and stare out into the dark night. Everything is still and quiet for the moment, but it isn't the comforting sort of silence. It's more like a sucked-in breath held tight, waiting for something awful to happen. "I hope Ezra's okay—and Dad, too."

Nate comes to my side and peers out the window. "Course they're okay," he says with a little too much enthusiasm. "Ezra basically speaks animal, and your dad's a park ranger. Didn't you tell me once that his job was pretty much the same thing as a superhero?"

"That was only to get you to quit talking about all of Brigadier Ajax's superpowers during math class." I wrap my arms around my knees, wishing we were all together again, safe and sound at the campground. Or better yet, back home in Shady Pines.

"We'll find them," Nate says softly. "You'll see."

"Thanks, Nate." Even if he's got no real way of knowing that things will turn out okay, it still feels good to hear somebody say it. I roll my neck and yawn. "You ready to get some sleep?"

Nate rubs his freshly bandaged arm. "Ready."

I click off the kitchen light, and we make our way to the back room. The air here smells heavier and dustier, like it gets a lot less use than the front room. I plop down on a bottom bunk. The blankets are thin and scratchy.

I open my journal, not wanting to forget about everything we've run into tonight.

Species Found at the Lab
Thermal vent worm
Extremophile bacteria—likes it hot, makes
sulfuric acid
Tiny translucent swimmers, blue fish, and
swirly stuff in petri dish
Desert scorpion
Who's behind it all?

I sigh and close my journal. In the distance, there's the faint howling of wolves. I pull the sheet over my face and think of Ezra. We may be surrounded by creepy crawlers, but at least they're all in jars. He's alone in the woods with whatever else lurks in the darkness.

CHAPTER THIRTEEN

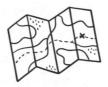

As the first rays of sunlight break through the windows, my eyes flip open. "Time to rise and shine," I whisper, and knock on the wood slats of the bunk above me.

Nate grunts something indecipherable and then rolls over again. He's not exactly a morning person.

I slide my bare feet to the floor and give a little groan. My whole body aches. I trudge into the cabin's tiny bathroom and clean myself up as best I can, then rewrap my ankle tight. All snug, it almost feels normal. My stomach grumbles, and I make my way to the kitchen. Maybe some breakfast will get Nate moving.

I find a box of crackers and a jar of peanut butter to make us a snack, but I can't find a knife. I open a kitchen drawer. It's got a stack of dried food packs. I consider grabbing those, too, but we've already done so much borrowing that I'm starting to feel like a bandit.

I pull open the next drawer, and beneath a pile of papers

I spot a small black electronic device with a tiny screen and loads of knobs and buttons. It's not a knife, but maybe it's a way to get a message out to Gramma and Dad. As I fiddle with the dials, Nate appears behind me, his finger dripping with peanut butter. "Morning," he mumbles.

"Ew, Nate. I was trying to find a knife."

He licks his finger and nods to the device. "What's that thing?"

"It might be some sort of high-tech walkie-talkie." I turn another dial. Static hums from the small black box. I hit a few more buttons, and a second later it starts making a faint beeping sound.

"Do you see any way to call out?" Nate asks.

"Maybe it doesn't have good enough reception." I shuffle toward the center of the room and the beeps get louder. I take a few more steps, then bump into my backpack. I lean forward to push it out of my way. The device goes wild. I scoot my backpack a few feet and the sound gets quieter again. I step toward the bag. Louder. I pull the zipper. On top of my journal and canteen, I spot the silver tracker I found in Dad's stuff. I lift it out. A light on the inside of the band flashes green, and the black box squawks as loud as a smoke alarm. "The black box must be some kind of receiver, and it's picking up signals from Dad's tracker."

"What does that mean exactly?" Nate asks.

I peer around the cabin. "There's no way this can be a coincidence. Dad must have something to do with this place."

"Maybe lots of park rangers have hideouts in the woods with creepy bugs in jars and surveillance gear. This might be nothing to worry about," Nate says in a voice that's supposed to be encouraging, but I can tell he doesn't believe his own spiel.

Nate screws the lid back onto the peanut butter jar and drops it into his backpack. "What do we do now?"

"We need to search this place and find out exactly what Dad's involved in." I click off the tracking device and hobble toward a silver filing cabinet near the wall of surveillance monitors. The top drawer is filled with paper clips, stacks of manila folders, and a disorganized heap of paper. It looks exactly the way Dad keeps his drawers back home. I pull out a file folder labeled *Chimera Project*.

"Chimera?" Nate asks, leaning in close. "I love those things."

"You know what a chimera is?"

"Don't you remember the summer after fourth grade when I was always drawing those three-headed creatures?"

I nod. "That was the year you were super into mythology."

"Ah, to be young again." Nate gives a wistful smile. "In Greek mythology chimeras are fire-breathing monsters that are part snake, lion, and goat. But comic books sometimes have chimeras too. In that case, it's not necessarily a three-headed beast. It just means a character's DNA has been mixed with something else to make a sorta hybrid creature."

Hybrids. I glance back at the folder, a wave of queasiness swishing around in my stomach as I turn the first page. There're pictures of the Komodo dragon, scorpion, little fish, plus a blobby, eight-legged critter with long claws and a tube for a nose. Based on the extreme magnification of the bit of plant life next to the creature, my guess is the picture was taken under a microscope. Something about the tiny feet and the wrinkly face look familiar. I flip the photo over. Written in messy blue ink is the word *TARDIGRADE.* I read an article a couple months ago in a *National Geographic* magazine about tardigrades. They also go by another name. "Moss piglet," I murmur.

"That's the ugliest piggy I've ever seen," Nate says. "I want one so bad."

"They're some of the scrappiest creatures on earth. They can survive in glaciers, in space, even volcanos. They're virtually indestructible," I say, and flip to another page in the folder. It's a shiny full-color printout that looks like some sort of advertisement. At the top are the words *CRISPR-Cas9-NHEJ* and an image of the double helix of a strand of DNA.

"Cas9," I murmur. "I've seen that before." I unzip the front pouch of my backpack and pull out the vial that I found in the snake trap. Sure enough, in tiny letters along the side is the same combination of letters.

"What does that mean?" Nate asks.

I scan the page, then read aloud. "'CRISPR-Cas9 provides scientists with a simple method to alter DNA, revolutionizing the future of genetic engineering. The applications for this technology are limitless. Using a protein called Cas-9, CRISPR works like a pair of DNA scissors allowing scientists to remove unwanted traits and insert new ones.'" I pause, trying to take it all in. If Dad is mixed up in this, then things are way worse than I ever imagined.

I read the last line. "'In short, with CRISPR technology it's possible to completely rewrite the genome and create scientific wonders the world has never seen.'"

"Whoa," Nate says with wide eyes. "Your dad is a biohacker."

"Biohacker?" I ask.

"Do-it-yourself biologist. I watched a thing on TV about it. People do all sorts of weird stuff. Putting tech under the skin that lets them start their cars without keys, or figure out which direction is north with a vibration in their necks. Maybe CRISPR modifications are the next level up."

None of that sounds like stuff Dad should be into. An achy feeling spreads through my chest. Dad says he's working on a way for us to all be together again—either him moving back home or getting transferred to an area of the park closer to schools for me and Ezra. But it doesn't look like he's been thinking about that at all. Instead, it appears his attention's been on a project that could keep us from ever being together again. I tug on the end of my ponytail. "Maybe Finn Brody was right about park rangers."

Before Nate can answer, there's a whooshing sound coming from somewhere above the cabin. I peek out the window. Just beyond the tree line, there's a red-and-white helicopter hovering in the sky. A voice booms out. "This is search and rescue. Repeat, this is search and rescue."

"We're getting out of here!" Nate shouts, and starts for the door.

I'm just about to bolt after him when I peer around the room. I freeze. If a rescue team picks us up here, they'll discover Dad's lab. The whole place is jam-packed with incriminating evidence. I'd always hoped Dad would leave Yellowstone and come back to Shady Pines, but if anyone else sees what he's been working on, he might be heading to prison, not home. I glance at Nate's puffy red arm. "You go and keep them distracted while I cover the place back up with the camo stuff. They'll fix your arm and I'll meet up with you after I find Dad and Ezra."

Nate looks at me like I've just told him he should give up *The Conspiracy Squad* and take up knitting instead. "You really think I'm going to leave you alone in an evacuated national park to solve a massive mystery all by yourself?"

"You're hurt. You need to go," I say as the sound of the helicopters gets closer.

Nate crosses his arms. "We're in this together."

I glance out the window again. The helicopter is moving higher in the sky. "Are you sure you want to do this?"

"I'm sure."

The helicopter veers to the left, making a wide arc over the trees. In another minute, the sound fades and the helicopter disappears from view. We're on our own again.

We finish packing our bags and refill on supplies, including some antibiotic cream for Nate's arm. I toss in the Chimera folder and the receiver I found in the drawer. And in case we need something sweet later, I empty a jar of hard candy from the kitchen into the side pouch of my backpack. When we leave the cabin, I carefully cover the whole place up with the leafy camo netting. We definitely don't need Finn Brody's film crew discovering the lab before we can make it back to Dad.

As we hike, I keep an eye out for Ezra, but no luck yet. We come to a fork in the trail. One way points to Shoshone Meadows three miles away and the other to a creek a quarter of a mile from us. If Ezra's still nearby, maybe he stopped there to cool off. "How do you feel about a little detour?" I ask.

Nate wipes sweat from his sunburned forehead. "It's my policy to never say no to swimming."

I crack a smile and we veer toward the path leading to the creek.

I search the banks and the woods surrounding the creek before deciding Ezra isn't here. I splash cool water on my face, then unwrap my ankle and dip my throbbing foot in. The softly flowing water eases some of the pain and I stretch out on a warm boulder along the banks to dry off. I pull out my journal and jot a few notes.

> Discoveries at Lab in the Woods
> The animal tracker from Dad's bag
> communicates with the receiver in the lab
> Dad may be using CRISPR-Cas9 to biohack
> animals' DNA—trying to make chimeras?
> Finn Brody might be right about park rangers
> keeping secrets

Nate lies flat on his back in three inches of water near the shore. His eyes are closed, and he'd look completely peaceful if it weren't for the pink flush in his cheeks and the red, puffy skin around his bite peeking out just beneath the bandage. The antibiotic cream isn't helping as much as I'd hoped. I rewrap my ankle and put my shoes back on. "We should get going. This trip's already taken us way too long."

Nate scans the wilderness, then gulps. "We might have another slowdown headed our way. Like, right now."

Nearby, trees rustle, and something shifts among the leaves. I struggle to my feet. "Is it the wolves? We're in no shape for a standoff."

"Could be," Nate says, getting to his feet.

I shift my gaze down and push off the boulder, bracing myself for the pain from my foot. I'm about to book it away from the creek when Nate says, "Wait a sec, Mags. That's no wolf pack. That's Ezra . . . and the gnarliest snake I've ever seen."

CHAPTER FOURTEEN

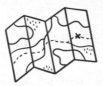

turn and face the direction Nate's pointing, then gasp. Draped over Ezra's shoulders is a hefty brown snake the size of a boa constrictor. On its sides are two yellow lumps that look like scaly golf balls.

"No way," I breathe. "That can't be the same snake he had yesterday."

"Looks like the little guy had a major growth spurt," Nate says.

As Ezra jogs our way, the snake ripples across his body and coils itself around Ezra's chest.

"Watch out, dude!" Nate squeals. "That thing's gonna crush your bones to bits!"

Ezra strokes the back of the boa. "No need to worry. He's friendly."

I push one hand through my messy hair. Ezra is talking nonsense. It was bad enough adopting the snake when it was tiny, but this is next-level nutty. "What happened to the snake? It's huge!"

"I don't know exactly. It just keeps getting bigger. Maybe it has something to do with whatever was in those syringes."

I study the snake. Not only are the yellow lumps bigger, but the snake's scaly skin is starting to look thin and crackly, like my leopard gecko back home gets right before he sheds it. If this is an example of one of Dad's genetically modified animals, the results aren't pretty.

I look back to Ezra. "Where have you been? We've been looking all over the place for you."

"I accidently dropped Slither back at the fumarole and had to chase him down for a bit. After that, I couldn't find you guys," Ezra answers.

"You named the snake?" I ask.

"I couldn't just keep saying, 'Hey, snake,' could I?" Ezra shrugs. "You doing okay?"

I cross my arms. If he hadn't run off in the first place, he'd already know how we were doing. "Nate's wolf bite is infected and I twisted my ankle. So, not great." I eye the hulking rubber boa. "What have you been feeding that thing anyway?"

"That's the weird part," Ezra says. "I've only managed to catch a couple of mice since we found him yesterday. I don't know how he got supersized overnight."

"I know exactly how it happened," Nate announces.

"You do?" Ezra asks.

"Ever hear of a little thing called CRISPR?" Nate asks, like he's suddenly an expert in the genetic editing tech we learned about an hour ago.

Ezra cocks his head to the side. "Should I have?"

"Only if you're keeping up-to-date with the latest in bioengineering," Nate replies, looking smugger by the second.

Ezra's gaze shift to me. "I'm not following."

"It's mostly bad news," I say, and update Ezra on the lab in the woods and what we read in the *Chimera* folder. "All the evidence points to Dad."

"So you're saying Dad's got a secret hideout and is using some crispy thing to mutate animals in the park?"

"It's called CRISPR . . . but otherwise, that's pretty much the gist of it." I nod.

"On the upside, that snake's new look proves your dad is basically the smartest guy on the planet. He's a total trailblazer," Nate says encouragingly.

"I don't think the authorities are gonna see it that way. Messing with animals' DNA is probably illegal and even if it's not, I'm pretty sure you can't release mutants into a national park without permission," Ezra says.

"That's why we've got to get to Dad before anyone else finds out," I chime in.

"Yeah, and unfortunately, we ran into the film crew that specializes in snooping out these kinds of conspiracies,"

Nate says, while unscrewing the lid to the jar of peanut butter.

"You guys got new snacks?" Ezra asks, eyeing the peanut butter hungrily.

"We loaded up at the cabin. Help yourself." Nate extends the jar to Ezra.

Ezra scowls. "It's got finger marks in it."

Nate peers down at the jar and then swipes a glob with his index finger. "So it does."

I open my bag. "We've also got more water, oranges, and some grapes."

"I'll take the food without finger marks." Ezra reaches for an orange.

"You ready to get a move on?" I ask. "The trail that leads to Shoshone Meadows isn't far from here."

"We're ready," Ezra says, and adjusts the snake on his shoulders.

I clear my throat. "You don't think we should maybe leave the snake here? He's a big boy now. I'm sure he can take care of himself."

"I'm not bailing on him just because he gained a bit of weight. I mean, look at the bumps on his sides. Who knows what's going on with all that? Until I know he's okay, I'm not letting him wander Yellowstone alone."

I bite the insides of my cheeks. I don't have anything against snakes, but we could really use Ezra's full attention to make sure this next leg of the trip goes smoothly. If we get lost again or run into any more creatures, things could go downhill fast.

We start down the trail, and after half an hour of hiking I stop and check the map. It seems like we're going the right way, but I've been wrong before. "Hey, Ezra, can you look at this with me?"

Ezra glances my way, then shifts Slither on his shoulders. "You're better at that sort of thing than me."

I refold the map. "This way," I say, hoping my guess is right.

We start off again, and the path narrows with brambles and tree roots cutting into the trail. The wind shifts. The smell of hot sulfur wafts around us.

"I know that stink," Nate murmurs. "Rotten eggs."

My gaze darts through the shadowy trees. We're not prepared for another attack. "Maybe it was just a gust from one of the thermal pools. Smells can travel a long way."

"Stink isn't the only thing that can travel." Nate jerks his head toward a cluster of reeds near the creek. A forked yellow tongue flicks out. "It looks like Captain BiteyPants just can't get enough of us."

The Komodo swaggers out of the brush, swishing its colossal tail like a cowboy cracking a whip.

"How does it keep finding us?" Ezra asks.

I think back to what I know about Komodo dragons. "They're fantastic trackers and can follow a scent for miles. Maybe after it took Nate's flip-flop, it got a taste for people, and us in particular."

"We need to move," Ezra says, and grips on tight to Slither.

I sling my backpack on, and the three of us dash toward the dirt trail. With my ankle wrapped tight, only twinges of pain spark when my foot hits the ground. We run down the path, dodging hunks of rock and tree branches. This area must've gotten hit pretty bad by the last earthquake. It's nearly impassable. I steal a glance over my shoulder, hoping the obstacle course is slowing down the lizard. The Komodo dragon zooms after us, running with its lopsided trot. Its mouth opens wide, and stringy drool flings from bright pink gums.

We leap over a pile of rubble, then skid to a stop. A stone's throw ahead, steam rises from an orange-and-teal thermal pool. To the right is a steep drop-off and to the left a barricade of rubble. The pool burbles as wafts of steam rise into swirling clouds. "It's a dead end." I spin around, searching for any way out, but every path is blocked.

Nate tugs my arm. "Mags, we got a problem."

"I know," I say, closing my eyes and trying to calm down

the panic swirling through my gut. "Just let me think for a second."

"No, I mean we've got an ultra-mega-huge problem." Nate nods to the thermal pool.

I turn. The water ripples, and five pairs of golden eyes with dark green heads rise from the steamy surface.

CHAPTER FIFTEEN

At first I think they're just small Komodo dragons, but something isn't right about their bodies. Their tails don't lie flat. Instead, they're segmented and curl upward toward their heads, just like a scorpion's tail. And their skin. It isn't exactly scales. It's smoother and shiny, like the crunchy exoskeleton of a beetle.

The lizard . . . scorpion . . . things skitter our way. They're forest green and the size of coyotes with jaws that drip with foamy drool. One twitches its tail, and a hissy rattle follows.

Ezra takes a step back. "What are they?"

"Scorp-ards—or maybe lizar-pions?" Nate whips out his camcorder. "We might be dead meat, but this is solid gold footage. If we survive, *The Conspiracy Squad* is gonna be the number-one-ranked channel of all time."

"You won't be getting any footage if your camera ends up in the belly of one of those things," Ezra warns.

The original Komodo dragon, Captain BiteyPants,

emits a low moaning sound, and the smaller creatures make an odd chirping hiss in response. These must be the babies that hatched by the fumarole. BiteyPants seems like a mostly normal Komodo, so if these are her kids, something very weird has happened to their DNA. The *Chimera* file said CRISPR let scientists rewrite the genome and create scientific wonders. But these things look more like nightmares.

The largest of the creatures is nearly the size of a wolf, with sharp yellow claws that scratch against the dirt as it moves. It passes a clump of sage. Something twitches in the brush. The lizard strikes with its spiked tail, and a clump of gray fur sprays out from the sage. A second later, the hybrid tears apart a limp rabbit.

"That's mega-nasty." Nate gulps.

They only hatched a couple days ago, and they're only a day old, and they're already hunting. "Creatures like this might explain some of the weird stuff Penelope's noticed in the park," I say.

"Hopefully, she got out of here with her little sisters before they had a run-in. These guys don't look friendly," Nate says.

"We need to get out of here too." My eyes dart to the trees. There aren't any branches low enough to climb, and the gaps between the hybrids are too small to try to scoot past them.

"One deadly reptile in the park was really enough. This is just overkill," Nate says, and launches a handful of pinecones at the snapping jaws of the chimeras.

One smacks a hybrid in the mouth. It clamps down on it and crushes it flat. Ezra dodges another while shielding Slither with his arm.

"At least they're not full-grown," I say. But as their spiked tails bob, I think about how hamster-size piranhas can gnaw a carcass to the bone in a matter of minutes.

With each launched pinecone, the hybrids move a little faster, their heads whipping round like sharks at the smell of blood.

"Quit throwing stuff. It's just getting them excited," I shout.

"What are we supposed to do?" Nate asks, holding a pinecone over his head like a grenade. "Lie down and let 'em thrash us?"

I think about my leopard gecko. Whenever I feed him live crickets, he gets way more hyper than when it's nothing but dried pellets. If we could remain still, maybe the hatchlings would lose interest. But as the lizard nearest Nate snaps at the air with a menacing hiss, I give up on that idea. The lizards are way too close for us to play dead and hope for the best. These guys are smaller than their Komodo dragon mom, but they've all got mouthfuls of razor-sharp teeth, plus the addition of the spiked scorpion tails. They're fast, venomous, and can apparently hang out in super-hot, acidic water and be just fine. I pick up a stick and hurl it at the closest lizard.

"So we're back to throwing stuff?" Nate asks.

The wolf-size chimera opens its mouth and shoots out a blast of steam.

Nate jumps back. "It breathes fire! I knew this thing was gonna end up being a real-deal dragon."

"It's not fire. It's st-steam," I stammer, as the puff of vapor heats my bare legs.

Slither ducks his head into Ezra's T-shirt, like even he's scared. "I'm gonna have to go with Nate on this one. That looks a whole lot like smoke."

"It's gotta be a reaction to coming out of the pool," I say, pushing down a wave of panic.

"Whatever it is, I don't want to get a shot of it in the face." Nate launches two fistfuls of acorns. A few peg the smallest chimera in the snout.

At that, the mother Komodo scuttles close to her young, a low groan rumbling in her throat. The hatchlings shift her way, imitating her sounds but in a slightly higher pitch. My gaze pivots to the trail beyond the thermal pool. With all the reptiles gathered in one place, the path is clear. If we're fast, we could make it.

I look to Nate and Ezra. They see it too.

We skitter past the thermal pool and are nearly home

free. My clenched muscles start to loosen the tiniest bit. Then something yanks me back. The wolf-size chimera has spun from the banks and clamped down on the bottom of my bag. I push forward and grab onto the tall weeds near the pool. But the lizard is strong and when it tugs again, I teeter back.

"Drop your bag!" Ezra shouts from the trees.

I start to slide the straps off my shoulders, then remember it's got nearly all our food and water, Nate's medicine, plus the map to get to Dad.

"Let the lizard have it already, Mags!" Nate yells.

Instead I reach into the side pocket where I stuffed the hard candy from the cabin. I toss out a big handful, hoping the chimera would rather eat them than my backpack.

The hybrid's segmented tail pulses up and down, inches from my neck. I duck. The butterscotches, peppermints, and cinnamon candies plop onto the lizard's still-wet skin instead of into its mouth.

I strain forward and grasp a boulder a few feet from the pool, then kick one foot into the lizard's side. But it's no good. The lizard's scales are like armor, and it doesn't even flinch when I make contact. If I want to avoid getting eaten, I'm gonna have to sacrifice my backpack.

I'm just about to ditch it when a syrupy smell wafts up. The chimera's skin has turned black where the candy fell, and a curl of smoke rises off its neck. The hatchling flicks out its tongue, tasting the air, then shakes its body, throwing off the candies. They land in the pool with a *splunk*. The water bubbles and tubes of coal black twist and curl up where the sweets landed.

The lizard opens its jaws in a hiss, and my bag slips out of its mouth. I scramble away from the banks. The chimera rattles its tail and dives away from the smoking black puddle on the surface.

I race to Nate and Ezra at the edge of the wooded trail. We run from the water until we're far enough away to take a breather. When we come to a stop, Ezra grabs my arm. "You almost got yourself roasted over a backpack."

I unzip my bag and pull out the map. "We've already been lost for two days. My compass is broken, and Yellowstone is massive. I did what I had to."

Nate ruffles his curly hair. "That was intense. And what was up with that water? It looked like it started to grow those black snake fireworks we light at Fourth of July."

"I think it was some kind of chemical reaction with the candy. The lizard didn't seem to like it either," I say.

"Next time you have to choose between being eaten or losing a map, ditch the map," Ezra says sternly, then adjusts Slither on his shoulders and starts for the trailhead. As he walks, I notice he's not going as fast as usual and he keeps twisting his neck and rubbing one shoulder.

"That snake is too heavy. It's going to slow us down," I say.

"I'm fine. And he's not just any old snake. His name is Slither." Ezra grunts, then picks up his pace.

Nobody's acting the way they're supposed to anymore. Dad's gotten himself tangled up in some bizarre experiment. Ezra would rather haul around a thirty-pound snake than help Nate and me figure things out. Even the animals aren't themselves. I can't make a plan when everything is upside down. As we hike past low hills, gurgling mud pots, and tall, skinny pines, the park seems bigger. It's too wild and unpredictable. With each turn into a new patch of forest, I feel smaller and more exhausted.

Every now and then, the earth gives a little rumble, and far-off mountains groan. An uneasy tightness builds inside me. We should have come to a trail marker by now, but we haven't. They're probably all buried under piles of rubble.

When we reach a bit of rocky trail, Nate stumbles.

"Do you need a rest?" I ask. Between Nate's bite, my hurt ankle, and Ezra shouldering Slither, none of us are moving very fast.

Nate shakes his head and rubs one hand over his arm. Even with the antibiotic cream, the skin around the bite is still pink and swollen, and a few angry red streaks fan out from beneath the bandage.

"If I sit down, I'm pretty sure I won't get up again anytime soon."

I give him a long look. His clothes are torn and covered in dirt, and his eyes are ringed in dark circles. "You need medicine. Like, real medicine. From a doctor."

"It's not so bad. I'm turning into a werewolf, remember? Comes with the territory." He tries to crack a smile, but it looks more like a grimace.

"Except none of us really believe that," I say.

"I'll be all right, Mags. Let's just keep going."

On and on we go until I lose all track of time. Every few minutes, I glance over my shoulder at Nate. At first he'd give me an encouraging nod or a tiny smile, but now he doesn't even meet my eye. Ezra's still in the lead, but his pace is more of a trudge than a march.

I'm so tired that I can't think straight anymore. I've stopped wondering whether we're going in the right direction. All I can do is focus on lifting my feet up and down.

"Almost there," I say, even though I've got no real idea if we're getting closer or farther.

When the path winds into a grassy meadow, Nate's the first to stop. He grips his arm, and his face scrunches into a scowl.

"Want some more Tylenol?" I ask, reaching for my backpack.

Nate wipes one hand across his forehead but doesn't answer. I open the bottle and hand him the pill. "You've got water in your canteen to take it with, right?"

Nate gives a slight nod, swallows the pill, then closes his eyes.

"The infection's getting worse," Ezra says. "He needs a doctor."

"I know that," I whisper. "And if you weren't so busy trying to rescue random animals, you could spend more energy helping me figure things out."

Ezra dodges my glare. "You seemed like you had stuff under control."

I don't bother keeping my voice low this time. "How does any of this seem like I have a thing under control? We're lost, hurt, and being chased by hybrid animals. But all you care about is that snake."

His face colors. "I like the snake. Okay? I want to keep it safe too. Is that a problem? Maybe I'm different from you. From everybody. Did you ever think about that?"

"What does that even mean?" I throw my hands up in the air, sick of Ezra's moodiness. "I'm sorry that you had a bad experience in the woods this summer. Really I am. But you're better now. You can snap out of it already."

"You don't know if I'm better. You're not in my head."

I bunch my hands up, but before I can get the next round of words out, Nate's knees go limp and he starts to fall. I slide my arm under his back and catch him as he crumples to the dirt. After a few seconds he blinks and then meets my eye. "Oh. Hey, Mags. Guess I decided to take an impromptu nap."

I hand him the canteen, feeling guilty that I didn't notice he was about to crash.

Nate takes a drink, then peers from me to Ezra. "You guys done fighting yet?"

"We're done." I look over my shoulder at Ezra. He adjusts Slither and turns away, his jaw set hard. We might have quit arguing, but we're not done being mad.

I touch my hand to Nate's head. He's way too hot. "Let's rest for a minute and give the pills a second to kick in."

Nate lies back in the grass. "I'm just spitballin' here, but what if I didn't get bit by a wolf?"

"You definitely got bit," Ezra says, standing several yards away from me and Nate. "Those wolves were practically on top of us."

"But they weren't the only thing out there," Nate says.

"You mean the Komodo dragon?" I ask, feeling Nate's eyes digging into me.

"What was that you told me about the dragon's mouth being filled with gunk?"

"They have a venomous bite," I say, thinking of the thousand-pound moose taken down by the Komodo. If that's what got Nate the other night, we're in real trouble.

Nate closes his eyes. "I remember something about a slow, agonizing death."

"That's not going to happen," I say. "We'll get you to a doctor and get you taken care of."

"Would that be before or after we hike all over earthquake lava-pool central?"

"We'll carry you if we have to," Ezra says, but I question how much he really means that since his hands are a bit full with the mutant snake.

Nate struggles to a sitting position, and a bead of sweat runs down his forehead. "I'm ready when you are."

I pull the map from my bag and study the trails. Everything needs to go perfect from this moment forward. "Shoshone Meadows is less than a mile from here. The path's marked easy, so as long as we don't bump into any more disasters, we should make it there in half an hour."

Nate chugs another mouthful of water. "Too bad disasters are this place's specialty."

We start down the trail again, Ezra at the front. The path is smooth and free of the debris we've bumped into elsewhere. I take a sip from my canteen and look out toward the blue-gray sky. The sun is sinking low now, and the temperature's already dipped noticeably. I tuck my arms close to my body as we pass the final trail marker, pointing us to the spring. In a matter of minutes, we'll reach our final destination. But I'm not sure what we'll find once we get there. We haven't talked to Dad in two days, and since then, we've learned about the Chimera Project and come face-to-face with the genetically modified monsters in the park. The best I can hope for is that he's still here, in one piece, and able to give us some answers.

"This is it," Ezra calls.

There's a sign for the Shoshone Meadows campground just ahead. I break into a run, ignoring the pang in my ankle.

There's a smoking campfire, a canvas tent, and a yellow mare tied to a tree—it's Daisy, Dad's trail horse! Only he said she ran off when we first spoke to him two days ago. It doesn't matter now. Dad can explain it all later. I spin to Nate and Ezra, a smile stretching across my face. "We made it."

CHAPTER SIXTEEN

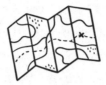

I run the rest of the distance to the campsite, calling for Dad the whole way. But there's no answer. We split up and check the creek and woods nearby. Piles of rubble and broken tree branches are scattered over the ground from the recent earthquakes.

At last, I head back to the campsite, hoping maybe he went to pick berries or get water and can't hear us calling him. The sun drops behind the tree line. It'll be dark again soon.

I pause by Daisy and give the horse a few pats on her muzzle. We've come all this way and if Dad isn't here, then not only was all our hiking a waste, but now we're even farther from civilization and in much worse shape than when we started. As I wait for Nate and Ezra to get back from searching, I lean my face against Daisy's mane, wishing she could tell me everything I want to know about Dad. Instead, she swishes her tail and gives a low whinny.

All of a sudden, Ezra breaks through the woods

surrounding the campsite and heads my way. He's holding a ripped piece of gray fabric in one hand. "I found something!"

As he gets closer, I recognize a familiar brown badge on the torn cloth—an embroidered evergreen tree, a grazing bison, and the words NATIONAL PARK SERVICE. The fabric is the torn-off sleeve of a park ranger's uniform.

I scan the shadowy edges of the woods. "Any sign of Dad?"

"No, but I found this next to the sleeve." Ezra opens his other hand, revealing a clump of long gray fur. An image of the snarling wolf pack flashes through my mind.

"The wolves. They were here," I say, a wave of despair washing over me.

"We don't know if they got near Dad. His shirt could've gotten torn in the quake," Ezra answers, but stress lines tug between his brows.

"Last time we talked to Dad he was hurt. If he ran into them, it could have been bad."

Ezra shifts Slither on his shoulders and peers over the campsite. "The horse is okay. That seems like a good sign."

I look Daisy over. It's true. A hungry pack of wolves would have definitely attacked a tied-up horse.

"We're not alone after all!" Nate's voice calls from down the trail. As he speeds our way, he waves both arms, grinning wide.

Ezra smiles. "See, I told you we didn't need to worry."

But instead of Dad following at Nate's heels, it's Finn Brody and the rest of the film crew.

My heart sinks. I need Dad. Not the conspiracy theory documentarians.

"Look who I bumped into down by the creek!" Nate says, practically dancing with glee as he heads our way.

"You guys are still here? And you're at our campsite?" Finn asks, flicking one hand through his spiky blond hair.

I shake my head, trying to put the pieces together. "But that's my dad's horse and the last time we talked to him, he was here."

Finn shrugs. "The horse showed up this afternoon. We don't know where it came from. We gave it food and water and figured somebody might come around for it. But there wasn't anybody here when we set up camp this morning."

"I thought you kids were heading out of the park like two days ago," Maki adds, setting down her fuzzy mic.

"We were planning to, but we haven't been able to find my dad," I say, and wrap my arms around myself.

"But we did find this," Ezra says, holding out the torn sleeve. As he moves, Slither extends his tongue and tastes the air. "You haven't seen a park ranger in a torn uniform by any chance, have you?"

"That's some snake you've got there," Finn says, and exchanges a curious look with Jake, then glances back at the sleeve. "We might have seen him. A few hours ago the camera caught a ranger hiking alone in the distance. We called out to him, but he was too far away to hear us."

"Did he look hurt?" I ask.

"He had a limp, but that was all I noticed," Finn answers.

"Could you tell where he was headed?" Ezra asks.

"He was moving through the backcountry, not on any trail. Maybe he was looking for you guys," Finn answers. "I'd let you call him, but my cell doesn't work all the way out here."

"We brought a walkie-talkie, but it got wet and quit working," I say with a sigh. I'm glad to know that Dad may be okay, but I'd feel even better if I knew where he was now. Just before the walkie gave out, I told him we'd head to Shoshone Meadows. I wish he'd waited here for us. But Dad's been doing a lot of stuff that doesn't make sense lately. Maybe he's more like the park rangers in Finn's documentaries than I wanted to believe. For a second, I wish I could ask Finn about them without raising suspicion, but then I'm not so sure I want to hear it. What if he tells me that all the rangers he's met over the years end up leaving their families to chase Bigfoot or join secret societies dedicated to keeping national park secrets?

"It's getting dark. You guys can stay here for the night, have dinner, then we'll help you find your way out first thing tomorrow," Maki says with a sympathetic smile. "This place isn't safe for kids."

"Tell me about it," Nate agrees, plopping down on a log by the fire. "I got bit by a dragon and Maggie was nearly drowned by a mutant scorpion lizard monster, then you got Ezra's new pal over there growing like nobody's business."

"It's got a rash or something?" Finn asks, eyeing Slither with a look that's somewhere between disgust and admiration. The snake and its bumps are still getting bigger, and the skin around them has already started to peel in long, thin strips. I wish Ezra would just let him go already, but the weirder Slither looks, the more attached Ezra seems to get.

"We found him in the woods. We're not sure what exactly is wrong with him," Ezra says vaguely. I'm relieved when he doesn't offer Finn any details about the trap or the CRISPR syringes.

"Well, if you get tired of watching him, let me know. I'm good with reptiles," Finn says, his artificially aquamarine eyes twinkling.

"Maybe later." Ezra shifts ever so slightly away from Finn.

Jake grabs a fabric ice chest hanging from the bear pole at the edge of camp. After two days in the park, his spray tan is looking a little streaky. He returns to the camp circle and gets the fire going again. "Hot dogs sound good to everybody?"

"Better than good." Nate grins.

Finn tugs on one of his ear piercings and turns to Nate. "Tell me more about this mutant scorpion thing. That definitely sounds like something I need to know about."

I grit my teeth, hoping Nate will stay tight-lipped, but instead he opens his backpack with a grin. "I can do better than that. I've got the whole shebang on video."

I shoot Nate a warning glare. If Finn finds out too much, his team might uncover that Dad's the one behind the monsters. But Nate doesn't even notice me and is already starting up the video. He's too starstruck to remember to be careful.

As Finn watches the footage, Jake roasts the hot dogs over the open flames. They sizzle and pop and my mouth waters. I rub a hand over my forehead. My skin is gritty with days of grime, and bloody scratches crisscross my legs.

I peer over at the camera as the screen shows the hybrid Komodos coming out of the thermal pool. "There are so many of them. And those tails. Incredible," Finn murmurs. "I'd kill for video like that. So far we've only been able to get shots of the Komodo dragon and a few shadowy things lurking in the woods. No Bigfoot and definitely no hybrid monsters."

"You could use some of my footage if you want," Nate offers, looking like he'd happily give Finn Brody all his camera gear and maybe even a kidney if he said the word.

"I might take you up on that if we don't get lucky in the next few days. I've been making documentaries for a while, but cash is running low. I need proof cryptids exist, or this film might be my last."

"No way!" Nate exclaims. "Your films are epic. Fans all around the world count on you. You can't quit."

"Thanks, man." Finn gives him a wistful smile. "Hopefully, it won't come to that, but I've got some pretty big skeptics back home. The only way they're gonna be convinced my work isn't a joke is with irrefutable proof."

On-screen, the lizards stalk toward us and Nate hurls a pinecone, then a moment later there's the footage of the creature nearly pulling me into the steaming water. Nate managed to zoom in enough to get a pretty good shot of the black stuff bubbling up out of the water.

"What's all that gunk?" Finn asks, leaning close to Nate's video camera.

"Some chemical thing with sugar, right, Mags?" Nate asks.

"It was hard candy. When it hit the water it grew those black tubes," I say, figuring it can't hurt to tell them that.

"You shouldn't have gotten so close to the pool," Maki says, peering up from what appears to be a hefty chemistry textbook. She shakes her head at the screen. "The fact that those creatures can survive in it says a lot about their body chemistry. We'd all die in a matter of seconds in water with that low of a pH."

We learned a little about pH in our chemistry unit last year. Mr. Guernsey gave us little papers to dip in stuff like dish soap and lemon juice to see if it was acidic or alkaline.

Maki motions to one of the black curls on-screen. "The pool is likely high in sulfuric acid. Which would explain why it reacted with sugar and made those carbon snakes you see there."

Nate grins at Maki. "Carbon snakes? That reminds me of when Brigadier Ajax faced off with some serpentine baddies on Planet Farentine. Do these snakes eat souls by any chance?"

Maki looks from Finn to Nate with a bewildered expression. "They're not real snakes. It's just a chemical reaction."

I think back to the specimens at the cabin. The thermophilic bacteria's label said it thrived in hot, sulfuric water. If some of its DNA was mixed into the hybrid lizards, that could explain how they survive the thermal pool's hostile conditions.

Finn laughs. "Leave it to Maki to ignore the monster in the water and only pay attention to the chemistry. On top of being an amazing sound engineer, she's working on a PhD in biochemistry. She's ten times smarter than me or Jake, but she's been putting up with our nonsense since our undergrad days anyway."

Maki smiles and pushes a strand of purple hair away from her face. "Jake cooks a mean hot dog and you keep things interesting. Besides, I can only do so many experiments in the lab before I have to get out in the field and live a little."

"Speaking of my amazing hot dogs, they're done," Jake announces, waltzing our way with a plate loaded with roasted weenies.

I take my first bite. The flavor explodes over my tongue, and I give a satisfied sigh. It feels incredible to eat a hot meal after so many huckleberries. I polish the whole thing off in less than a minute. Jake sets me up with another without me even having to ask.

Nate picks at his hot dog, then goes quiet. He slumps lower on the log seat, and his teeth start to chatter.

"You cold?" Finn asks. "I've got an extra jacket in my pack."

Sweat glides down Nate's neck and his eyes are glassy.

"I think he's going to need more than a jacket," I say. "He was bit by . . . an animal two days ago. He needs medicine."

Maki sets her plate down. "Pull off the bandage and let me have a look."

Nate hesitates, then slowly tugs on the edge of the bandage. I pull in a breath. The skin underneath is oozy, tinged green, and super swollen.

"Yikes," Ezra says, and pushes his hot dog away.

"I'm no medical doctor, but that's definitely infected," she says with a frown. "I have a bottle of antibiotics I brought in case of emergencies. It might not be the right thing for an animal bite, but it's better than nothing."

Maki reaches into her messenger bag and pulls out a small container of pills. "Take two now and another two in the morning, keep at it until the bottle's empty. When we get you back to town, a doctor can sort the rest out."

The sun sinks down, spreading red and orange streaks across the sky. I feel a little jab of guilt thinking about how I didn't want Nate to bring Finn and the others around. But they've done more to help us in a couple of hours than anybody else in the last few days.

"Thank you," I say, looking at the crew. "For everything."

"No prob, kid. We're just trying to do our good deed for the month." Finn grins.

As the others finish eating, I pull out my journal and jot down a few notes.

Chimera Project Mysteries
Wolf fur and Dad's torn sleeve near Shoshone Meadows

Film crew may have spotted Dad in the
forest—where was he headed?
"Carbon snakes" created by chemical
reaction of sugar and sulfuric acid
DNA from heat—loving creatures might help
lizards withstand boiling hot acid bath

I shut the journal and wonder what Dad's doing right now. Is he thinking about us? Or is he more concerned with his creations?

Finn slaps his knee. "Looks like the mosquitoes are back."

"Not again," Jake answers, looking more worried than you'd expect from a guy with so many muscles. "Every time one bites me, my eyes swell up and I'm itchy for a week. I think I'm allergic."

There's a faint whine in the air. I tuck my journal back in my bag, ready to slap any mosquitoes that zoom my way.

Maki tosses Jake a can of bug spray. "Squirt on another layer. You'll be all right."

Jake douses himself in the repellant, then lifts another dried branch onto the campfire. Ezra offers Slither a raw hot dog, but the snake only nudges it with his snout then recoils away. Nate yawns and nods off by the fire.

The first few stars blink in the night sky, and I rub one

eye, wondering if it's too early to say I'm ready for bed. Small crackles flit in the nearby brush, then the whining sound picks up again.

A trembling cloud buzzes out from the shadowy forest. Jake grimaces. "What is that?"

I squint to make out the shape in the light of the fire. It shifts and rolls our way like a tumbleweed caught in the wind.

"Oh, dang!" Jake leaps to his feet. "This isn't going to be pretty."

The high-pitched hum grows louder as the cloud blows closer. Only it isn't a cloud at all. It's a swarm of mosquitoes, each the size of a hummingbird with needle-sharp mouths as long as toothpicks.

CHAPTER SEVENTEEN

The insects churn in a whirling storm. Jake aims the can of bug spray and blasts the mosquitoes. But instead of retreating, they disperse, sending smaller clusters toward each of us.

I swing my backpack at a trio while Nate swats at a pair dive-bombing his face. Ezra tries to fend off his own cluster, but Slither writhes and snaps his jaws, making it impossible for him to keep his balance. Ezra tumbles to the dirt, and Slither uncoils himself from Ezra's body and starts to zigzag away.

"Help!" Ezra calls, looking frantic. "Slither's escaping!"

"We've got bigger problems right now!" I shout as a mosquito lands on my calf. Before I can shoo it away, it jabs its swordlike mouth into my skin. I gasp as the mosquito's almond-size belly starts to fill with my blood. I scream and kick my leg out. It breaks free and skids in the air toward Maki.

She ducks and spins to face Finn. "You said we were

going to see Bigfoot! Not overgrown mosquitoes. I didn't sign up for this!"

"I've got it under control!" Finn shouts back, but instead of doing anything helpful, he whips out his video camera and pans over the swarm.

"They're everywhere!" Jake screeches as a mob of mosquitoes circles his face. His cheeks are puffed up with bites and his eyes are swelling shut.

A clump of mosquitoes tumbles Finn's way. "On second thought, we better give these things some space." He shoves the camera into a case and takes off running for the woods. Maki and Jake follow.

I sling my backpack over my shoulders and turn to Nate. "You feel good enough to run?"

He nods. "Nothing like some mondo-size bloodsuckers to put a little pep in your step."

I bolt after Finn, Nate at my side. Ezra's already made a break for the woods in search of Slither. When we come around a bend in the trail, I spot Finn ducked behind a scraggly bush. He yanks what looks like some kind of handheld bug zapper out of his bag.

Nate and I slide to a stop next to him. "What is that?" I pant, hoping his bug repellant is more potent than the stuff Jake and Maki are using.

"Something to slow these guys down." Finn aims the zapper at the zooming insects. There's a popping sound, but nothing shoots out. The horde twitches but instead of falling out of the air, they whirl together faster, then zip through the woods like somebody just gave them all a big gulp of an energy drink.

Nate eyes Finn's zapper with a worried glance. "I know you've got loads of experience with weird creatures, but is that supposed to happen? 'Cause if I didn't know better, I'd say they seem faster, not slower."

Finn punches the side of the zapper. "This is what happens when you have a tiny budget to work with."

Just then an especially large mosquito drones our way. It's swollen from feeding and flying slower than the rest. Finn points the zapper at it and pulls the trigger. "Take that!"

The mosquito does a loopy figure eight, then drops out of the air with a plop. Finn pumps his fist. "That's what I'm talking about."

Nate gives him a high five. "Sorry I ever doubted you, man."

Finn grins. "This isn't my first rodeo. When you've bumped into as many strange things as I have, you come prepared."

"Nice work," I say, and let out a relieved sigh. Now if Finn can just do that a few dozen more times, we'll be rid of these monster-size mosquitoes.

But before Finn can home in on the next target, a

rapid, high-pitched whine kicks off. The downed mosquito zooms up from the dirt. Its movements are jerky and way faster than before. It aims its daggerlike mouth and speeds our way.

Finn tosses the zapper into his bag. "It's back! We gotta run!"

The others come around the bend, panting and smacking their arms and legs. A mosquito zips toward Jake, who's already got both arms wrapped tight around his face and a look of dread in his eye. "Noo!" he yelps. The supercharged mosquito jabs its sharp probiscus into the tip of Jake's nose. Within seconds, Jake looks like he's wearing a bright red clown nose.

Nate yelps and hurries after Finn. Ezra calls for Slither, but must have realized running off in the woods solo was a bad idea because he's now scrambling after Jake and Maki. I'm about to follow them when I hear a whinny back at the campsite. Dad's mare, Daisy. The mosquitoes will eat her alive if she stays tied up.

I race through the woods back to the campsite. Daisy shakes her head and whips her tail as mosquitoes circle her. I dodge them as I hurry to untie her from the tree. When she's free, she rises up on her back legs with a wild snort, then gallops toward the dirt trail.

The mosquitoes give up on chasing Daisy after a few yards, then regroup to swarm after me. I take off for the woods in a frenzy of swatting and dodging the insects. Some of them are so fast they have to be from the first group Finn hit with the zapper. Their whine is a nonstop sawing in my ears. The bite on my leg feels like it's on fire. But if I stop to scratch for even a second, the insects will be all over me. All I can do is pump my legs and hope the mosquitoes will run out of steam before I do.

Wings flick against my cheek and their shrill hum drones in my ears. I run harder, leaping over brambles and dead logs as I go. Within a few minutes, the sound grows fainter. I keep going. Not thinking about anything except escaping the whine and their sharp mouths. At last, my legs give way under me and I have to stop. My lungs burn and I gasp for air. I drop to the forest floor and finally take a look around me. The last bits of light have faded and the woods are nearly swallowed up by darkness. "Nate? Ezra?" I call.

My voice echoes after me. I pull my flashlight out of my backpack and shine it over the unfamiliar ground. There's no sign of the others. A current of panic shoots through me and I spring to my feet.

I call out for Nate and Ezra again, but the only response is a mournful wolf cry in the distance. Skeletal branches rattle in the trees overhead.

A cold wind blows and I shiver. I'm alone and more lost than ever.

CHAPTER EIGHTEEN

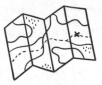

The woods close in around me. I raise the flashlight and shine it over the trees. There's a snap and a pop. I spin around. The shadows form gruesome shapes. Anything could be out here. Wolves, grizzlies, more genetically modified monsters. My feet start moving again though I don't know where I'm going anymore. I shout for the others until I'm hoarse.

A faint buzz picks up in the air. I strain my ears. There's a definite whine to it. The sound grows louder and the trees above stir. A familiar whoosh, whoosh. Not the nagging whine of the mosquitoes . . . but the roar of a helicopter. I point my flashlight at the sky. In the distance, I can make out the gleam of spinning metal blades. I wave my arms and shout at the top of my lungs. But surrounded by miles of trees my voice feels tiny. The helicopter pivots to the right. I can't let it get away.

I turn and race through the woods in its direction. Tree branches slap my skin and snag my clothes as I follow the fading sound. I move faster shining my light as high into the sky as I can. If someone up there would just glance my way, they'd have to see its beam. But as I tilt my face to the treetops, I see that the flashlight's glow doesn't even make it past the canopy. Yellowstone is huge, and I'm only a tiny speck. I slow my pace. The terrain is rough, and my feet constantly catch on bits of forest debris. Something sharp jabs at my foot, tearing the fabric of my left sneaker. I wriggle my foot. Two toes poke out of the dirt-stained shoe.

At last, all traces of the helicopter's roar vanish, and I can't see anything in the sky but the moon and the first few stars. Tears well in my eyes. I'm too tired and beat up and lost to keep running. The rescue team is gone. My ankle throbs, and the scratches and cuts on my arms and legs sting.

I collapse on the ground and close my eyes. I'll have to sleep out in the open. Alone and defenseless. I don't know what else to do. The temperature's dropping quick. I pull my knees to my chest for warmth. Earlier, it felt like things were starting to go our way. Nate got medicine. We had a hot meal and grown-ups who were going to help us out of the park. But I've lost all that now.

I wrap my hands around my ears, trying to block out the creaks and scratches of the forest and imagine myself back in front of the flickering warmth of the campfire.

A faint beep joins in with the rest of the sounds of the woods. I squeeze my eyes tighter. Even if it was a dozen rescue planes, they probably wouldn't spot me way down here anyway. But the beep doesn't quit. It gets louder. I sit up with a groan and tilt my head. The noise is coming from my backpack. I unzip it and fish out the receiver I took from the lab. It squawks and three bars flicker across the screen.

The last time it went off it was because of the ankle tracker in my backpack, but I turned that band's power off when we left the cabin. The most likely explanation for the sound is an animal with a tracker nearby. But there's a small chance the receiver is picking up on a person in the area. Maybe a scientist carrying a tracker. Maybe even Dad. Either way, I'd rather go after whatever it is than wait around for it to find me.

I struggle to my feet, feeling as worn out as my torn sneakers. It's like a game of Hot or Cold. A step the wrong way and the bars and the beeps start to vanish. In the right direction and they're loud and clear again. At last, the beeps get steadily stronger, and my flashlight beam glints off a structure up ahead. Just off the trail, there's a wooden building with a metal garage door. It's about the size of a two-car garage with a rolling door that's cracked open a foot at the bottom. Shelter.

A laugh mixed with a sob bursts out of my mouth. I

limp-run to the building. The lights are all off inside, but the beeps keep getting louder.

I bend and tug the door the rest of the way up. Inside, the room reeks of fertilizer and gasoline. There's a chain hanging from a single light bulb in the center of the ceiling. I tug the cord and a dim ring of light chases the thick blackness away. There are rows of shelves stocked with spare parts, tools, and cleaning supplies. I scan the garage looking for a landline phone or some walkie-talkies. Instead I spot drop cloths and a familiar backpack on the floor near a cluster of rakes and shovels. I rush to the makeshift bed. Dad must have spent a night here. But I don't know why he would've left his things. I call out for him just in case, but I'm not surprised when there's no answer. The place has a lonely feel, like no one's been here for quite a while.

The beeps have stopped, so I pick up the left-behind map. It's got a trail marked and an unnamed pond circled. There's a mud cauldron to the west of it and a fossil forest to the east. I survey the empty garage, wondering where Dad was headed and why.

Something scuttles in the far corner of the garage. I jump to my feet. "Dad? Is that you?"

There's more scuffling. I can barely make out the outline of a pair of gray jackrabbits in the shadows. A wave of relief spills over me. I can deal with rabbits. "It's okay. You can come out. I won't hurt you," I say, and kneel to grab my flashlight.

The light falls on two crouched animals.

I step back. These aren't jackrabbits. At least not exactly. Long slender horns protrude from each of their fuzzy heads. A smile breaks over my face. When I tell Nate about this, he's going to freak out. They're jackalopes and they're adorable.

I open my backpack and slowly pull out my last orange. I quickly peel it and then hold out a piece. "Here, bunny. You hungry?" Their soft gray noses twitch, and one takes a few tentative hops closer. The jackalopes are big, around the size of small dogs, with long ears and legs.

I stretch my arm out farther, letting the bit of orange lie on my open palm. The jackalope approaches. Its antlers gleam in the light. It closes the distance between us and tilts its head to take the piece. Its mouth opens and I catch a glimpse of glistening white fangs. There's a throaty growl and I jerk away as the jackalope snaps at my fingers. It misses them by a fraction of an inch. I scuttle back. Both jackalopes leap my way, antlers thrust out, ready to gore whatever crosses their path.

I race across the garage. The rabbits bound after me at lightning speed. I hit the wall as one springs in my direction, bashing a hole into the Sheetrock with its antlers. As it struggles to free itself from the wall, the other bolts my way. I can't keep up this pace. They're too fast and I'll tire out before they will. I turn and squat with my arms extended in front of me. When the jackalope springs again, I'm ready. I grab its antlers with both hands. It snaps its fangs at my face, but I raise my arms and hurl the rabbit out the open garage door. It's surprisingly heavy for a creature so small.

I race to the jackalope still stuck in the wall, yank it out by its back legs, and throw it as far as I can out into the woods. A banshee howl pierces the night as the jackalope flies through the air. I dust my hands off, feeling a twinge of pride at taking out two ferocious bunnies.

I'm just about to heave the door down when I spot something skulking out of the woods. The receiver beeps louder than ever. A hybrid Komodo dragon the size of an alligator slinks my way.

I dart for the garage door and yank. It doesn't budge. Maybe that explains why it was left open in the first place. The creature slides under the open door and into the garage. The receiver in my backpack screams. There's a silver band around one of the lizard's ankles. Someone—maybe Dad—must have put a tracker on the hatchling, too.

The hybrid takes another lopsided step my way. Stringy red drool and fluffy gray bunny fur cling to its open mouth. I cringe and scan the shelves for anything I can use to keep from ending up like the jackalope. I spot a shovel hanging on the wall. I grab it and swing it in front of me. "Get out of here!"

Instead, it whips its stinger at my feet and lets out a low hiss. I smack the shovel down on its snout but it doesn't even blink. Up close, the creature's dark scales have an iridescent green glow and look shiny and crunchy instead of rough and dry like normal reptiles. Even its scorpion tail isn't quite normal. It's transparent and speckled blobs of liquid swirl beneath the hard exoskeleton. It reminds me of videos I've seen of microscopic amoebas. I shudder, wondering what kind of bizarre DNA soup was mixed together to make this thing.

The hybrid bashes my legs with its head, and I stumble into the shelves that line the walls. Paint cans and hand tools rattle. I swing the shovel again, but with the lizard so close I can't get enough momentum to do any damage. It ignores my whacks and thrusts its tongue out, tasting the air. The hybrid could bite me now and rip off my leg, but I think it's toying with me. Like when my cat gets ahold of a grasshopper and tosses it up in the air. Just before he bites the thing's head off.

I scan the shelves in search of a new weapon. I spot a fire extinguisher just above my right hand. I stretch to grab it, then pull the safety latch and point the extinguisher at the chimera. White foam blasts out, covering the hybrid in a layer of froth. The lizard blinks slowly and I unload another cloud.

The can runs dry and I launch the empty container at the creature. It bounces off its back and falls to the ground with a clank. My whole body trembles, and I can barely see through blurred eyes. The chimera gives a shake like a dog after a bath. Foam flies off its scales.

It bangs its head into my calves again. I hit the shelves harder this time. Screws and paint brushes rain down, bouncing off the hybrid's scaly armor. Another shove and my legs give way. I hit the concrete ground and land inches from the dripping jaws of the monster. Hot egg-scented breath stings my eyes. Its mouth is wide open and tears slide down my cheeks. There's no way I can fight this thing with my bare hands, and there's no time to come up with a backup plan.

There's a creaking sound and the shelves teeter for-ward. A bag tumbles from the top shelf and crashes to the ground. White powder explodes over us. The hybrid hisses and recoils its segmented tail. It wriggles its body like a colony of fire ants is biting its skin.

I read the label. It's a twenty-pound bag of borax. Back home, Gramma sometimes uses the stuff for cleaning laundry. Apparently, it's also kryptonite for the hybrids. This just might be my way out. I kick the bag and more powder puffs out, coating us both in even more borax. The white stuff sizzles on the hybrid's scaly skin. It skitters back with another hiss. I grab a handful and hurl it in the creature's face. Its reptilian eyes twitch, then it turns and scuttles out of the building and into the darkness.

I sprint to the door, but it's still jammed. I peer up and notice a push broom has fallen forward and gotten stuck in the garage door's track. I grab the shovel and whack the broom down. I give the door another tug, and this time it rolls closed easily.

I press my ear to the metal door and listen. When all the twitches and snaps in the forest finally fade away, I exhale. I cross the garage and sit down on the pile of drop cloths by Dad's stuff. The material is scratchy and thin enough that I can feel the cold against my legs. After everything I'd seen in the park the last couple of days, I didn't think things could get any worse. But I was wrong. Being alone makes everything a thousand times scarier. When I close my eyes, I can't get rid of the sharp-fanged jackalopes and the rattling tail of the mutant Komodo.

I can hardly believe I'm still alive. I glance at the dusty pile of borax powder by the wall of shelves. Somehow that stuff saved me.

The lizard has way tougher skin than me, but when the powder touched it, it sizzled and burned. I study my dusty white legs. I'm coated in borax and yet I'm fine. Which means there's something about the borax that hurts the hybrid but not people. After we watched Nate's video, Maki said the pH in the thermal pools was so acidic it would kill other creatures. But the chimeras weren't bothered. That means the lizards thrive at a different pH than people. What if the borax was the opposite of acidic— alkaline—and that's why it caused such a bad reaction for the lizard, but not me?

I rub one hand over my forehead. I can't think straight anymore, but I'm too wired to try to fall asleep right now. I lean over and unzip Dad's backpack. Inside, there's loose papers, a flashlight, and a brown leather book. I lift it out. Like me, Dad's always kept a journal. I open it and inhale, but the pages smell like ink and glue, not Dad. I flip to an entry dated a week ago.

August 10, 5:30 p.m.

Had another unusual sighting today. This time it was a cage out in the middle of nowhere. The thing was empty but there was fur and oddly enough scales, too. I can't figure out who would have put it there.

I chew at my thumbnail and flip to another entry.

August 12, 12:33 p.m.

I could have sworn I saw an alligator in the park today. I talked to my boss. He said I'm spending too much time alone. I don't want to make a scene about it. Not after everything that happened at my last job. I know the kids are counting on me to hold things together here.

There's another entry lower on the page from the same day.

August 12, 9:15 p.m.

Tonight didn't go as planned. I know I said I was going to keep my nose out of trouble. But when I was out on my rounds, I found an animal tracker and another trap. It was rigged up with a bunch of needles. I don't know what was in the syringes, but if I tell my boss, I'm pretty sure he'll think I've jumped off the deep end. I might not get that promotion and then I'll never be able to bring the kids out to the park like I planned. I'm not sure what to do, but I can't let this slide either.

I press one hand against my temples, turning the pages faster to an entry from the day before we arrived in Yellowstone.

August 14, 1:30 a.m.

The kids arrive tomorrow morning. I want it to be a great week for us, but I've got a lot on my mind. Something strange is definitely happening in the park. I can't confide in my boss and I can't tell the kids. They've been through enough already.

I'll have to handle it on my own.

CHAPTER NINETEEN

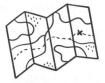

The cold concrete pulls the heat from my body and I shiver. My head swims with the words in Dad's journal. Nothing I've read sounds like Dad was some big mastermind behind everything we've encountered so far. In fact, it seems like the opposite. Dad didn't know what was happening and he was scared. The tracker in his bag wasn't his. But I was so quick to believe it was evidence against him. I should've known better than to think he'd do something so reckless.

I pull in a shaky breath and turn to the last entry in the journal. It's from this morning.

August 18, 6:45 a.m.

I've got no way to get in contact with the kids, and every hour things seem to get a little worse in the park. I waited as long as I could at Shoshone Meadows, but last night I had a run-in with a pack of wolves. It was a narrow escape. At least I found shelter for tonight, but I wish more than anything that the kids were here with me. I can't panic now or I won't be any good to them or myself. They're smart kids and they're together. They'll take care of each other. I've got to trust that and focus on doing my part. I'm going back to the place where this all started. Maybe I can find whoever left the trap there in the first place and get some answers.

The place where this all started. Dad must be heading to the pond I saw marked on the map. But judging by all his left-behind gear, he rushed out in a hurry. Something must have scared him off. I just have to hope that he got away in time.

I read over the last entry again.

They'll take care of each other.

An achy tightness spreads over my throat. Dad believes in us and is counting on us to pull together and get through it. He isn't the one responsible for this mess, but he's working hard to try to fix it.

I lie down between the drop cloths and pull the scratchy fabric to my chin. I can't give up now. I don't know how yet, but I'm going to find a way to help Dad.

All the running and fighting of the day finally hits me. My eyelids slide shut and everything fades away.

Sunlight floods into the garage from the lone window on the side of the building. It's been three days since we left our campsite and started off on our own, but it feels like so many more. I sit up and stretch. My back hurts from sleeping on the concrete, and my legs are itchy and sore. But the sinking weight that made me want to give up is gone. I want to find Dad and tell him that I'm sorry I didn't trust him and that I've got his back. He's out there alone up against who knows how many chimeras. I glance at the bag of borax powder on the ground. A few handfuls got rid of last night's hybrid. What could a whole bag do?

I find the garage on the map and run my finger to the pond Dad circled. It's nearly two miles away. And around here, two miles could mean running into a million different disasters. But there's one hazard I'll be prepared against. I cross the garage and grab a wheelbarrow. It's made of thick green plastic and is lightweight but sturdy. I hoist in the mostly full bag of borax. My empty stomach rumbles as I tug my backpack on and drop the map and Dad's journal inside. I don't know what's around the corner. But this isn't over yet. There's got to be a way we can turn this whole thing around. I push the door up and squint as light floods my vision.

I eye the sun's position. It's still pretty early. Hopefully, this hike goes better than the last few times we've hit the trail. With the way the chimeras have been growing, I need to make it to Dad in a hurry or we'll be up against Godzilla-size predators soon.

I start hiking, my stomach feeling hollower with every

step. I wish I hadn't wasted my last orange on the jackalopes. I take a swig of lukewarm water to try to fill a bit
of the emptiness. After a few more minutes of walking,
the woods get denser. In the tangles of green, I spot a
huckleberry bush and push the wheelbarrow its way. But
when I get closer, I see the bush is nearly bare. Only a few
overripe ones are left squished and rotting on the forest
floor. My belly rumbles, and for a second I consider eating
the fallen huckleberries but decide food poisoning won't
help my situation.

I turn back for the trail. A branch behind me rustles,
then wings soar just over my head. They're dappled with
white and tan spots like a hawk, only the body isn't a bird's.
It's a writhing brown snake. I stumble backward and fall
into the huckleberry bush.

I'd accepted jackalopes and scorp-ards, but I don't think
I can handle flying snakes. I try to army crawl behind the
wheelbarrow for shelter, but the snake-bird dive-bombs
me, and its scaly tail grazes the back of my neck. I scream.
I've been hiking less than an hour and I'm already under
siege. This mission is doomed.

There's more rustling in the brush. I throw my hands
over my head and hold my breath. If there's a legion of
flying snakes coming for me, I'd rather pass out now than
feel any more cold scales brush against me. Wings beat
the air and my head gets fuzzy.

"Knock it off! You're freaking her out!"

Hurried footsteps beat the ground. There's a snort, and I peek up from under my arms. Ezra and Nate peer down at me with big smirks on their faces.

"No need to freak out, Mags. He's not gonna hurt you." Ezra laughs.

I leap to my feet and am about to tell Ezra he can wipe the grin off his face right now or I'll do it for him, when the snake-bird lands on a tree branch just above Ezra's shoulder. It tucks its wings in and coils itself tight around the wood.

"Good boy, Slither," Ezra says.

I shudder. "That's not Slither. That thing is a winged menace."

"Slither's a growing boy," Nate chimes in. "Those bumps on his sides sprouted last night. I guess that's why he ran off for a bit. Pretty nasty, but that's mutants for ya."

I give Slither a wary glance, then turn back to Nate and Ezra. Now that I'm over the shock of the flying snake it finally hits me. I charge toward Nate and wrap my arms around him and squeeze, then dash to Ezra and do the same thing. "You're here! You found me!"

Ezra shoves me away with a grin. "We were all out looking for you when we heard somebody screaming. Nate and I took off running. Finn and the others will be coming around soon too," Ezra says.

"Anybody would scream if they saw a winged snake," I mutter, and dust bits of dried leaves and twigs off my shorts.

"At least it wasn't a flying spider. Now, that would be a true abomination," Nate says. I notice his face isn't as pale and his eyes are clearer.

I smile. "Your infection is getting better."

"I took my second dose of medicine around sunrise. I'm starting to feel like my old self."

Ezra eyes the wheelbarrow loaded up with borax. "Traveling kinda heavy these days, aren't you, Maggie?"

"A lot has happened since I last saw you guys. I spent the night in a garage, but I wasn't alone. I bumped into one of the hatchlings. It's gotten much bigger in the last twenty-four hours. I would have been dead meat if it weren't for the borax. When it touched the hybrid's skin, it freaked out and ran off. I also had a run-in with a pair of jackalopes. Those things are cute but deadly."

"Dang." Nate's jaw drops. "We're apart for one night and I miss out on all the fun."

"I wouldn't exactly call last night 'fun'. But I did learn more about what's going on with Dad. I found some of his stuff in the garage, including his journal. He isn't the one behind the mutants. He's been investigating them this whole time."

Ezra looks relieved for a moment, then worry returns

to his face. "You found his stuff but not him? Where'd he go?"

"According to his journal, he's headed to a pond a few miles from here. He's trying to save the park. And I'm going to help him. That's what the wheelbarrow is for." At that last bit, I raise my chin, ready for Nate and Ezra to try to talk me out of going after Dad.

"You're not going by yourself," Ezra says with finality.

"Ditto that," Nate adds.

Before I can argue, Ezra starts again. "Once the crew catches up, we'll all go. We're staying together the rest of this trip. You've got no idea how much we were freaking out last night. We thought you might be dead." He gives me a long look. Traces of fear linger in his eyes.

I peer up at him. "That's how I felt when you vanished."

Ezra lets out a big whoosh of air, then pushes one hand through his dark hair. "I haven't been the best brother on this trip. I should've been paying more attention. Making sure you were safe." Then he glances at Nate. "Both of you. But I guess I thought you liked being in charge, Mags. You love organizing stuff. I didn't think you really needed my help."

"Just because I like having a plan doesn't mean I wanted to tackle all this on my own," I say, not ready to let Ezra off the hook.

Ezra looks up at the sky, as if he's searching for the

right words to say. "I've been pretty caught up in thinking about how nobody understands me lately, at least nobody human. Sometimes, I don't feel like me. Or even know who 'me' is supposed to be anymore. Like, I notice stuff I didn't before, animals for one thing."

"I like animals," I say. "There's nothing weird about that . . . well, maybe taking care of cockroaches and hauling around a genetically modified snake is a little weird, but a lot of people like unusual creatures. They end up being vets or working at zoos."

"She's right," Nate agrees. "My cousin Ricky has a pet boa constrictor and gets paid fifty bucks just to bring Sheila out to kids' birthday parties. Not a bad gig."

Ezra shakes his head. "It's not just the animal thing. It's other stuff. Like, the music I used to listen to doesn't sound as good and I don't even like the same food. Plus, the last couple of times I hung out with Jack and Zion everything felt off. I guess that's why I like Slither. He knows what it's like to be different."

I nod. Ezra isn't the only one changing. A year ago, pecan pie used to be my favorite, and now it makes me queasy. And last month I had Gramma cancel my *Ranger Rick* magazine subscription, and I used to love that thing. But before I can tell Ezra any of that, Finn, Maki, and Jake bustle through the brush loaded up with all their camera equipment. Like us, they're looking rougher from their days in the park. The black cat tattooed on Jake's arm is so puffy from mosquito bites that it looks more like an overfed panther.

When Finn spots Slither wrapped around the tree branch, he grins and pushes one hand through his bleach-blond hair. "I got that snake's first flight on film. Nobody's gonna doubt cryptids are real after they see this footage."

Nate taps the camera hanging from his neck. "I got some shots too. Hope you don't mind a little friendly competition."

"Just as long as mine goes up first," he says coolly.

"Enough about the video." Maki turns my way and wipes one hand across her forehead. Her purple hair is twisted up in a messy half bun and she has dark circles under her eyes. "We've been searching all over the place for you. I hardly slept last night. But you're alive, that's what matters now." She opens her pack and hands me a water bottle and two granola bars. "I'm guessing you're hungry?"

"Starving." I tear into the package and polish off the first bar in seconds. I wipe crumbs from my mouth, then meet Maki's eyes. "I'm sorry I scared you guys. I went back to help the horse and after that I got lost. I ended up staying the night in a garage that my dad had just been in." I update the crew on how Dad's investigating the mutants in the park and our plans to help him. Now that I know

Dad's not involved, I don't mind sharing a little more of the story with Finn's crew.

"What exactly did your dad say about the cryptids?" Finn asks, his fingers flicking at a silver chain around his neck.

"Not a lot . . . mostly that he was worried." Something about the sharpness in Finn's eyes keeps me from saying more.

"Can we tell them about the lab in the woods now?" Nate asks.

"I don't think—"

"What lab?" Maki asks.

Nate taps his camera. "We've got evidence right here that the monsters aren't natural. They're man-made."

Maki comes closer. "Man-made?"

Finn shifts his body between Maki and Nate. His normally calm and cool expression has suddenly morphed into extreme agitation. Warning bells go off in my head. "That's a nice theory," he snaps. "But I've been researching cryptids in the national parks a very long time, and whatever you think you found in the woods is more proof that the rangers are hiding something."

Nate wrinkles his nose. "But Maggie's dad—"

I grab Nate's arm and give him a meaningful look. "Don't worry about it, okay? We probably don't have all the facts just yet."

Nate looks confused, then shrugs and says, "Well, you guys are the experts, I guess."

"We'll help you get to your dad. Maybe he can answer some questions when we meet him." Finn rubs the back of his neck. As he stretches, a pendant on the silver chain slips out of his shirt—a three-headed creature—lion, goat, and snake.

I tilt my head. Back at the lab, Nate mentioned a three-headed creature from Greek mythology.

It was called a chimera.

CHAPTER TWENTY

Which way do we go?" Finn asks, looking impatient.

A chill skates down my spine as Finn tucks the pendant back into his shirt. The lab files on biohacking animals were all a part of the Chimera Project. And Finn's wearing their emblem. This time, I'm sure it's no coincidence.

I slowly open the map, but instead of pointing to the pond, I shift my finger to the right and motion toward a mud cauldron surrounded by a wooded area.

"That's not too far from here. We'll be there in an hour or less." Finn checks his compass and starts off on the trail. Maki and Jake follow. My heart hammers as I lift the wheelbarrow handles.

"What's that for?" Maki asks, glancing back at the bag of borax.

"The hybrids don't like it," I mutter, but my mind's not on the wheelbarrow. Maki doesn't look quite satisfied, but

ATTACK OF THE KILLER KOMODOS

she shrugs and starts walking again. I slow my pace. Finn needs cryptids to be real. Without them, his documentaries are a bust. Last night he admitted he was running short on cash and that he had lots of skeptics back home. If he was desperate enough, how far would he go to make sure his next film was filled with creatures the world had never seen before?

Nate slides by me, pointing his video camera at a grassy meadow on one side of the trail. "Regular ol' grass or UFO landing site? You decide."

I need to get Nate and Ezra alone. If Finn and his crew are the ones behind the Chimera Project, this changes everything.

I tug Nate's arm. "Wait," I whisper, then call to Ezra in a louder voice. "I think it's time one of you helped me push the wheelbarrow. I'm getting a crick in my neck."

Instead, Jake turns, his muscles bulging out from his dirt-stained muscle shirt. "Need a hand?"

"No!" I snap, then force myself to speak in a calm, soothing voice. "I mean . . . we've got it under control. Thanks anyway."

When there's some space between us, Ezra arches a brow. "What was that all about?"

Slither glides a few feet above our heads. I try not to shudder when his scaly tail touches my ponytail. When the crew is far enough ahead to be out of earshot, I whisper,

"Finn Brody isn't just documenting weird creatures in the park. He's the one creating them."

Nate pshaws. "No way. Finn's a good guy. He's letting me add some video to his latest documentary and might even give me a line in the credits."

I peer at the film crew. The distance has grown between us, and they're nearing a bend in the trail. "We know somebody's biohacking animals in the park, and Finn's the most likely suspect."

Nate crosses his arms. "What proof do you have?"

"For starters, he's wearing a chimera necklace, which was the project name on the files we found in the lab."

Nate's face colors. "That's not proof. It's a coincidence. Loads of people dig mythical creatures."

"There's more. I'm pretty sure that zapper thing is some sort of DNA gun. He used it the other night on the mosquitoes and afterward, they got faster," I say. "Plus, Maki's a chemist. She probably filled him in on all sorts of stuff about making mutants that can thrive in sulfuric waters."

Ezra glances at Nate. "He *is* pretty obsessed with finding an undiscovered species. And if Dad's not the one behind the experiments, it has to be someone else."

"Have we considered extraterrestrials?" Nate suggests. "They're always messing with people for no good reason."

"I don't think we can blame this one on aliens," I say.

"Just think about it. Finn's reputation depends on the existence of cryptids. He said himself that unless his latest documentary proves their existence, it'll be his last. He has a motive."

"But having a motive doesn't mean he could actually do it. I'm guessing making hybrid monsters isn't the easiest thing in the world," Ezra whispers as he maneuvers the wheelbarrow around a jagged rock.

"That's where the CRISPR tech comes in," I add, keeping my voice so low Ezra and Nate have to lean in close to hear. "The paper at the lab said it worked like a pair of DNA scissors that let scientists get rid of certain traits and add new ones."

Ezra tilts his head, considering. "But still, Finn's a filmmaker. Do you really think he'd know how to use something like that?"

Nate swallows. "His PhD in molecular genetics might've helped a bit."

"What?" I hiss so loud Maki glances over her shoulder. I force a smile and give a little wave. She turns back around and I whisper, "Why didn't you mention that part earlier?"

Nate shrugs guiltily. "I figured it meant he was a smart guy. I never thought the world's coolest documentary filmmaker could be a baddie."

Ezra glances up to where Slither glides overhead, a conflicted expression on his face. "That means Finn's responsible for creating him too."

Nate offers an encouraging smile. "Even if he was made by a villain, it doesn't make him evil. All sorts of comic book heroes are created by some pretty messed-up circumstances."

"What we need to focus on now is getting away from the crew and making it to Dad. If we show up at the pond with Finn and he sees Dad, it could be bad. Finn might try to pin everything on Dad for his documentary," I say.

"Dad definitely doesn't need another scandal coming his way," Ezra says. He looks genuinely concerned. Maybe he really is starting to come around and think about his family again. If the three of us were able to work as a team, we just might be able to figure this thing out.

Nate clenches his jaw. "It's one thing to investigate Bigfoot and jackalopes. It's a whole other deal to create them yourself. People are getting hurt. That crosses a line."

"Everything okay back there? You guys are moving pretty slow," Finn calls. The sunlight catches his aquamarine eyes and all I can think of is the white wolf and its cold glare.

"Just pacing ourselves. Be there in a sec." Nate waves.

"What's our move?" Nate asks. "They know where we're going. Even if we escape, they'll just find us later."

"I pointed to the mud cauldron, not the pond," I admit.

"Stealthy move." Nate nods approvingly.

I glance up at Maki. She seemed worried about me when I went missing. For a moment, I feel sort of guilty to run away again, but then I remember that she's a part of Finn's crew. With her background in chemistry, she's probably just as responsible for the monsters in the park as he is.

"Getting away isn't going to be easy, especially considering we're hauling around a wheelbarrow," Ezra says.

"Maybe we all say we need a bathroom break and then bolt into the woods instead," I suggest.

Nate wrinkles his nose. "Who takes a wheelbarrow with them on a potty break?"

"Who goes to the bathroom in a group?" Ezra adds.

I sigh. "Okay, maybe that's a bad idea, but we need to think of something."

"I've got it," Nate says, his eyes flashing. "Keep moving and I'll catch up with you in a minute." Nate unzips his backpack and tugs out a gray sweatshirt borrowed from Finn. "Go," he urges as he kneels and starts fiddling with his shoelaces. Ezra and I walk side by side blocking Nate from sight. A few more seconds pass, then Nate whispers, "I'm ready."

I glance over my shoulder. Nate holds the lump of gray fabric sectioned off by his shoelace into three misshapen wads. A pair of twigs protrudes from the top blob.

"What is that supposed to be?" I ask.

Nate's brows dance up and down. "A decoy. We'll tell them we spotted a jackalope and while they're checking it out, we bail."

"I don't think they're gonna fall for it, man. It looks like dirty laundry," Ezra says.

Nate examines his creation. "I guess it is pretty lumpy."

We're almost to the fork in the trail where we'll need to turn to go to the pond instead of the mud cauldron. But there's no way we can make a break for it without it being totally obvious. We're either going to have to tell the others that we're walking the wrong way or waste time heading to the mud cauldron instead of finding Dad.

I take another slow step, trying to buy time to decide what to do, when Ezra smacks my leg hard with the wheelbarrow. "Hey, watch out!" I grunt, and kneel to rub the spot.

"I didn't do anything," he says, his body rocking side to side.

He isn't the only one swaying. The ground roils under my feet and I tumble forward.

Jake crashes into Finn. The duffel bag loaded with camera gear crashes to the dirt. "Not the cameras!" Finn cries. Maki takes several zigzagging steps toward the heap, only to lose her footing and fall into Jake and Finn. Rocky debris skitters down from a nearby incline in the trail. The crew shouts and tries to gather the equipment but keeps losing their footing.

It's total chaos.

If we're ever going to get away, it's now.

CHAPTER TWENTY-ONE

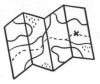

I reach for Nate and Ezra, grabbing on to them as the earth groans. "It's time to go."

Ezra eyes the path leading away from the film crew. It's bordered with evergreens that rain down pinecones and the occasional branch. The air is gray with dust. "We're going to get pummeled in there."

"Maybe not," Nate says. "I've got an idea . . . and this time I think it's better than the sweatshirt jackalope." He darts to the wheelbarrow, stumbling and tripping the whole way. He grabs the bag of borax and drops it to the ground. "Give me a hand!"

Ezra and I make our way to him. My stomach flips as the ground continues to quake.

"If we flip the wheelbarrow upside down, we can use it as a shield. Two of us can hold the wheelbarrow and one of us can manage the borax."

Ezra reaches for the bag as another violent current rumbles through the park, sending us crashing down again. As I struggle to my feet, I look to the film crew. Everything they'd managed to gather up in the last couple of minutes has scattered to the ground again. Their attention is fixed on the gear, not us.

Nate raises his arms up and takes the front of the wheelbarrow, Ezra moves to the middle with the borax bag clenched in his arms, and I hold up the back end of the barrow. We pivot to the trail that leads toward the pond. Moving like this is even tougher than I imagined. Sometimes Nate's steps are too fast for me and I nearly lose my grip. Other times, he slows down a bit and I ram into Ezra. On top of that, we can't really see what's ahead of us, just the trail under our feet. But when pings and thuds clack against the top of the wheelbarrow, I know we've hit the forest-lined trail and we move as fast as we possibly can.

After a while, the bumps die down and the ground feels more solid under my feet. "I think the quake has stopped," I say.

We cautiously lower the wheelbarrow and peer around us. The trail has wound away from the forest toward a meadow. Slither swoops overhead, his dappled wings spread wide as he soars. Ezra heaves the bag of borax into the wheelbarrow and grabs the handles. "We'd better pick up our pace before Finn and company realize we've left them."

We run for several minutes, passing a few antelopes grazing in the distance and a bubbling mud pot that looks like a
larger version of one of those fancy chocolate fountains you
see at weddings. The path opens up in front of us and we're
able to run three across on the trail. I'm feeling pretty good
about our progress until the dirt under my sneakers rumbles.
"Not another one!" I moan, and hit the ground.

Ezra and Nate flop down at my side. But instead of
shaking waves, there's the sound of galloping horse
hooves. I lift my head. It's a prairie wagon led by a beefy
brown horse and dad's yellow mare, Daisy. Penelope grips
the reins in one hand and waves her other arm. Samantha
and Tully squeal as they bounce up and down on the bench
seat at Penelope's sides.

"Looks like they got the wagon rolling again," Nate
says as we all scuttle back from the path.

"You know them?" Ezra asks.

"They're old friends." I smile.

The horses don't slow down even as they whip past us. I
squint to keep the clouds of dust out. The wagon's heading
for another bend in the trail. There are too many trees and not
enough room for it to speed through the place like a rampag-
ing buffalo. I jump to my feet and wave my arms. "Stop!"

Skinny branches whack the wagon's canvas canopy. Up
ahead, a low thick limb juts out onto the trail. "Penelope,
stop the horses!"

It's gonna crash.

But just before the chuckwagon smashes into the branch, the wheels dig into the dirt, and the horses skid to a stop. Penelope pops her head around the canopy and grins back at us. "How's it going?"

"That was a close one," I say, hurrying her way.

"I had everything under control." She casts a quick glance at her sisters. They're still gripping the bench seat tight. Penelope lets out a breath. "Okay, so maybe I'm a little new to driving, but I'll get the hang of it." She looks me over. "Did you get in a fight with somebody?"

I peer down at myself. My entire body is dinged up with bruises, gashes, and scratches. "A few somebodies, actually." I nod to the horses. "Your horse came back, and it looks like it rounded up my dad's mare, too. Does that mean you found your parents?"

Penelope rests the reins in her lap. "Not yet. The horses showed up together late last night, and we set off this morning. We were on our way out of the backcountry, then the earthquake hit. We had to change course and get on a clearer trail to avoid a mini-avalanche. Tully spotted you three in the binoculars, and we made another detour to see if you needed a lift."

"That's really nice of you . . . but we're actually not leaving just yet," I say.

Penelope glances from me to Ezra and Nate, who are

slowly making their way to the prairie schooner. Their arms and legs are covered in scratches and bruises, and their clothes are so dirty you can't tell what color they used to be. "What happened since I last saw you?"

"It's kind of a long story, but I think we figured out what's causing the birds in the park to act up," I say as Nate and Ezra join me.

Penelope leans forward on the edge of the wagon seat. "Fill me in."

I nod and hurry the words out, knowing every minute we spend here is another that Dad is out in the park alone. "Remember the Komodo dragon we told you about? Well, it isn't alone. It laid eggs in the park and they hatched. Only they're not normal lizards. Someone altered their DNA. They're part scorpion, part Komodo, part who knows what. That and there's some jackalopes and gigantic mosquitoes. They're all on the loose, and unless somebody finds a way to stop them soon, a lot of people could get hurt."

"Part scorpion?" Penelope asks, eyes shifting to Samantha.

"Told ya I saw a big lizard bug, Penny," Samantha says.

"It was dark, but whatever it was got too close to the chuckwagon last night. I unloaded the can of bear spray you gave us on it. It left us alone after that." Penelope gives a wary glance to the nearby woods, then scoots closer to her sisters on the wagon seat. "Got any ideas how the creatures got here?"

"There's this dude named Finn Brody who makes epic documentaries," Nate answers. "I used to think he was the coolest guy on earth, but it turns out he's an evil genius. He's got a top-secret lab hidden in the park, high-tech gear, and a whole load of creatures he's mutated into some pretty nasty monsters."

Penelope narrows her eyes. "Is this for real? Not some kind of joke for your YouTube channel?"

"I don't kid around about mutants. Especially those of the reptilian family," Nate says somberly. "If I were you, I'd clear out of the park pronto."

There's a glint in Penelope's eyes. "But you guys aren't leaving. You're headed straight for danger."

"My dad is at a pond not far from here. At least, I hope that's where he is. He's investigating the hybrids. We're going to help him," I say.

"I know this may sound mean, but how are the three of you going to stop a bunch of killer lizards?" Penelope asks.

I nod to the wheelbarrow. "The lizards were genetically modified to thrive in Yellowstone's acidic thermal pools. The wheelbarrow's filled with borax, which I'm pretty sure is a base. At any rate, when the powder touched one, it freaked out."

Penelope's eyes widen. "You got close enough to a mutant scorpion lizard thing to know that?"

"Scorp-ard," Nate interjects. "Or lizar-pion if you prefer."

I push a sweaty strand of hair off my forehead and give her a weary smile. "It's been a long few days."

Penelope studies me for a minute and then stretches out one arm. "Hop in and take a load off. We'll give you a ride to the pond."

"Are you sure? You're on your way out of here and the pond's in the wrong direction."

"If it was my parents out there, I know I'd want somebody to offer a little help. Now, get in."

I take her hand and squeeze in on the front bench next to Samantha and Tully.

Nate and Ezra load the wheelbarrow into the wagon, and Penelope clears a space for them to sit in back. When we're all inside, she grabs the reins and gives them a flick. "Hold on to your fannies!"

Giddy-up bolts forward, and I clamp my hands down on the edge of the seat to keep from flying out.

We make it to the pond even faster than I'd hoped, thanks to Penelope's scary-fast driving. At a trail marker up ahead, she stops the wagon, and Nate, Ezra, and I leap out. I peer toward a creek burbling near the trail. The early afternoon sun glistens off the water, birds sing, and the smell of pine needles drifts through the air. For a moment, the park feels so peaceful that I can almost believe everything's fine. There aren't any venomous predators lying in wait, and we're not dirty, beat up, and scared. But then my eyes shift to the creek's banks. Broken-off tree branches and heaps of rubble shake up the peaceful image and remind me that we need to stay alert.

Once we get the wheelbarrow unloaded, I make my way back to the front of the wagon. "I guess that's everything. Thanks for the ride."

Penelope rubs the reins between two fingers. "You sure this is a good idea? If those creatures are as dangerous as they sound, you guys could end up in trouble quick."

I stroke Daisy's muzzle. She gives a little snort and presses her cheek into my hand. I think about how Dad's journal entry said we'd take care of each other and make it through. He believes in us. Though we haven't exactly been a great team on this trip so far. With Ezra running off and me convincing myself that Dad had turned into some sort of mad scientist. Even Nate got caught up in his awe of Finn. But we've solved big problems before, and I think we could do it again if we tried. I look toward Ezra and Nate. "We'll find a way."

"For sure." Nate gives a sideways grin. "This isn't our first time wrangling mutants. We're practically old pros."

Ezra grunts. "I wouldn't go that far, but I think we'll manage. Especially now that we're all together again." His eyes hang on mine a moment.

I smile. I don't always understand him, but he's still my

brother and when it really comes down to it, he's got my back.

Penelope nods. "You wanna take your dad's horse with you the rest of the way?"

"Nah, she'll be safer with you," I say, and give the mare's nose another pat. "Besides, we'll get her back when this thing is over and we're all safe and sound."

She nods. "Well, good luck."

I wave.

"Don't go yet!" Samantha shouts, and scoots away from her big sister. "Me and Tully made a present for you!" She scuttles to the back of the wagon, then returns a moment later with a crinkled brown paper bag.

She hands it to me and I peer inside. There's slingshots and a bagful of saltwater taffies. "What's this for?"

"A snack and a shooter in case you bump into more lizard bugs. Load 'em up with rocks and whammy. They'll run off in a hurry." Samantha's eyes sparkle as she mimes pulling back the slingshot's band and letting a rock fly.

"Thank you." I smile at the two of them.

Nate rubs his hands together. "Got any root beer taffy in there?"

"A whole bunch!" Tully beams.

"We'll see you around." Penelope flicks the reins and the horses trot away. I grab the wheelbarrow's handles and we start down the trail. The air is thick with mist and the smell of sulfur. What should be a pedestrian-friendly path is littered with tree branches and jagged rocks.

As we keep going, I see why it's so muggy. There's a blast of water the size of a minivan shooting up near where the pond should be.

"Oh, dang," Nate murmurs. "More rocket water."

"You really think Dad's down there?" Ezra asks.

I peer toward the trail again, but the mist from the newly formed geyser makes it hard to see anything. "I hope so."

The farther we go, the wetter and hotter it gets, until finally it's so foggy I can't see my hand in front of my face.

"Does anybody else feel like we're walking through a ghost dance party?" Nate sniffs. "On second thought, I take that back. That stink is an insult to ghosties everywhere."

We move on and a faint rumble ripples over the earth. Aftershocks. At least they're not as bad as the big ones. I brace myself and keep going, avoiding a few rocks that skitter by. Dust mixes with the fog and I tuck my nose into my T-shirt.

As we near the pond, the geyser dies down to a burbling sputter and the air clears a bit. Slither glides overhead, occasionally dive-bombing the bushes and coming back up with a wriggling object in his jaws. A few more steps and I hear water lapping back and forth from the aftershock. The water comes into view at last. Only it's not some tiny swimming hole. It's a huge thermal pool ringed in so many brilliant colors that it looks like something out of a dream.

With each ripple, steam rises up from the pool. I don't see Dad anywhere around the thermal pool, but there're more wooded paths behind the water.

I head down the closest trail, calling for Dad and peeking into every cluster of bushes and thicket of trees. When we set out to find Dad three days ago, I thought things would be easy. We'd hike a couple of hours, maybe stumble upon an upended tree or geyser, but safely show up at Shoshone Meadows. He'd make a campfire and tell us stories. We'd laugh and create new memories and still manage to have a relaxing week in the park. But nothing's worked out the way I planned. Maybe Dad isn't even here anymore. Maybe the hybrids got to him before we did. There's a hot pang in my throat, and I give my head a shake. I can't think like that.

"Mags, over here," Nate calls. He's near the woods that border the thermal pool on the left side. "You need to see this."

I set the wheelbarrow down and hurry over to him. "Careful!" Nate waves his arms in warning.

When I reach him, I gasp. There's a massive fissure in the ground. At least fifty feet deep and twenty feet wide. "The earthquake created a ravine."

ATTACK OF THE KILLER KOMODOS

"And that's not all," Nate says, motioning to something inside the crevasse.

I squint. A dark figure shifts in the shadows of the broken rock. I drop to my knees at the mouth of the crevasse. "Dad!"

He limps into a sliver of light. My stomach churns. His face is thin and his clothes are torn and there's a bloody wound on his shoulder. "You shouldn't be here, Maggie. It's not safe! Something attacked me during the earthquake and I fell." His voice is raspy and strained.

I wipe my stinging eyes. "We're here to help you."

"You need to get Ezra and find a way back to Gramma as fast as possible. You can send rangers for me later. I'll be fine," he calls.

"We're not leaving you. I found your journal. I know about the hybrids and that you were trying to stop them."

Ezra jogs our way. "You found Dad?"

I motion to the crevasse. "We need to get a branch or something for him to grab on to."

"A branch?" Nate pffts. "We're not amateurs here." He pulls the rope with the grappling hook from his bag and starts spinning it over his head. "Maybe you could get a shot of me with the rope, Mags? Our sponsor would dig that."

"You have to go now," Dad calls.

I ignore his warnings and turn to Nate. "There's no

time for sponsored videos. Let's just find something to connect the rope to so we can toss it down to Dad."

"On it." Ezra dashes to a craggy boulder, probably thrown here by one of the recent landslides. Nate tosses the rope Ezra's way, and Ezra lodges the grappling hook into a groove in the stone. He gives it a hard tug. "That should hold."

"Get ready, Dad!" I toss the other end of the rope into the ravine. But as it spins down, it gets caught on a rock ledge. Dad peers up at the rope trapped several feet out of reach.

"Sorry! Can you still get it?" I call, my voice hoarse from all the shouting.

"I'll try," he answers.

Nate taps my shoulder. "Mags, we got a little situation."

"The hybrids?" I ask, dread sinking like a stone in my stomach as I scan the tree line.

But instead of skulking lizards, it's Finn, Maki, and Jake. Finn's aqua eyes are locked on us, his right arm stretched out pointing the zapper.

CHAPTER TWENTY-TWO

I hold my hands up in the air. "Don't shoot!"

"Finn, put that thing down. You're scaring them!" Maki orders. "You kids are hard to keep up with. After we lost you, we followed some horse tracks and they led us here."

Finn keeps the zapper held high, his eyes darting around the thermal pool. "I'm not going to shoot you, but you've come to the wrong place at the wrong time."

"We're here to help my dad," I answer. "You're the reason he's stuck down there. He's been trying to clean up your mess."

Maki looks confused. "Everything's going to be all right, Maggie. You just need some rest."

Finn tugs at a ring in his ear, then lowers the zapper. "I'm sorry about your dad, but we've got bigger problems. If my calculations are right, we're about to have a lot of company."

Maki pivots to Finn. "Company? What are you talking about?"

"Listen, I'm sorry I pulled you into this, but you know how much this documentary means to me. It has to be a hit or my career is over," he answers. "Without the creatures, there're no more films. I didn't have a choice."

The color drains from Maki's face. "Are you telling me you're responsible for the hybrids? But . . . how?"

Finn snorts. "My whole life people have underestimated me. I have a PhD and people still treat me like I'm some kind of underachieving hack. You want to know how I did it? I used my brains, a whole lot of willpower, and a few borrowed tools. You might be mad at me now, Maki, but when you consider the leap I made for science, you'll see things differently."

"You lied to me, Finn. Not cool." Maki turns and points the fluffy end of the boom mic at Jake. "Did you know about this too?"

Jake scratches at a mosquito bite on his earlobe. "I mostly just helped haul equipment."

Maki kicks the dirt. "I can't believe I let you two convince me there were actual cryptids in the park! My advisor was right. I should've taken the lab internship instead of wasting my summer with you."

Finn edges away from Maki, eyes pleading. "You know how my parents are. They don't appreciate my work, say I'm wasting my education. They were finally going to cut me off. No more cash. No more trips. I needed this documentary to work or everything I've done for the last ten years would be a waste!"

"So you made your own monsters because you couldn't find any real ones?" Maki screams, and smacks him again with the mic. "You're a jerk!"

"I'm sorry, okay?" Finn dodges Maki's blows. "After I got all the footage I needed, I was planning to fix the animals with the gene gun. Nobody was supposed to get hurt."

I nod to the zapper. "You can change the animals with that thing?"

"That's the plan. It's a biolistic particle delivery system. It fires DNA into cells, which lets me change what an organism is at its core."

Maki tilts her head, looking like she's temporarily forgotten to be furious with Finn. "I've heard of that before. In undergrad, a lecturer did a presentation on gene therapy. He injected DNA particles into plant cells. It made a fern grow quicker and bigger."

"Normally, it's a slow process, but I revolutionized the tech. Of course, I had to do a lot of experimenting first." Finn points to his own turquoise eyes. "Blue-eyed rainbow fish DNA."

"You experimented on yourself?" Maki asks.

Finn shrugs. "Nobody else was lining up to be my guinea pig."

Nate gapes at the zapper. "It's a magic sorcery shooter that lets you transform creatures into anything you want? Incredible."

"It's not magic. It's science," Finn replies. "Though, sometimes, it's hard to tell the two apart."

I narrow my eyes. "But what about the mosquitoes you shot the other night? They got faster and meaner."

Finn waves me off. "The device just needed a little more tweaking. I've already taken care of it."

I peer down into the crevasse, checking on Dad's progress. He's reached the end of the rope and has just started to make his ascent. I give him a thumbs-up, and he smiles faintly.

"We might want to take this convo elsewhere," Jake says, surveying the thermal pool warily.

I follow his gaze. A cloud of steam rises from the still surface. The water starts to churn and gurgle. A segmented tail emerges. Then another and another, until all five crocodile-size chimeras swish out of the pool. Their stingers glisten with water droplets, and their yellow and green scales shine like iridescent armor.

CHAPTER TWENTY-THREE

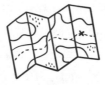

The hybrids creep to the shore, steam wafting off their backs in wispy clouds.

"What are you waiting for, Finn? They're coming. Use the gene gun already!" Maki shouts.

Finn aims the zapper, but his arms are shaking so much it'll be a miracle if he hits anything at all. Finn fires it at the nearest hybrid. "Take that!"

But there's no sudden transformation. Instead, the lizard saunters closer.

"Nothing's happening. Is it out of batteries or something?" Nate asks.

"This is a highly sophisticated biolistic particle delivery system for delivering exogenous DNA to animal cells. It takes time." Finn clears his throat. "But yeah. It's possible we're out of batteries." He taps a few more buttons, then shakes his head. "Nope, battery's good." He tries again, but still the lizards keep coming. "Small confession. I've never actually successfully reversed traits before. For some reason, it's a lot easier to add genes than to take them away. But in theory, it should work."

Maki shakes her head in disgust. "We're doomed."

Finn hits a few more buttons and fires several more times. The hybrids don't slow down. Finally, Finn groans and hurls the zapper. It skids across the dirt and lands with a thud. "This is what I get for buying discount merchandise off the Internet!"

I peek around the lizards to the other side of the thermal pool where I left the wheelbarrow. "There might be another way to stop the chimeras if we can get to that powder."

"The only way to do that is to go through the mutant lizard army or haul rump all the way around that massive pond of boiling stink," Nate says.

"I don't think that last one is gonna be an option much longer." Ezra points to the geyser. It's taller than any of us now and getting higher by the second.

If we do nothing, we'll be surrounded by the hybrids in less than a minute. After my encounter in the garage with just one, I know we can't let it come to that.

I suck in a big breath and take off running for the wheelbarrow while Nate, Ezra, and Maki shout for me to come back. The geyser churns out more water, and I have to make a wide turn to avoid getting splattered by the hot, acidic liquid.

When I'm almost there, I steal a glance back at the chimeras. Four of them still linger near the thermal pool, but one's scampered off in my direction. I sprint the rest of the way to the wheelbarrow, grab the handles, and turn to start back for the group. As I run faster, borax from the open bag flies out, coating my body in a thin layer of white.

I'm halfway to the group when the hybrid reaches me. The thermal pool blocks me in on one side and the forest lies on the other. I only have one option. I push the wheelbarrow toward the woods and away from the approaching reptile. I'm nearly to the tree line when a cluster of mosquitoes fans out from the gloom of the woods. Their noxious whine fills the air.

I turn to dodge the bloodsuckers, which sends me right back to the Komodo hybrid. Its tail is raised high, and the stinger is aimed square at my middle. I glance to the others, ready to call for help, but they've got troubles of their own. The four other lizards have them circled.

I'm on my own.

I stretch my fingers toward the wheelbarrow, trying to grab hold of the bag of borax, but before I can make contact, the chimera whips its tail, knocking both me and the wheelbarrow over and sending the borax splattering to the dirt.

Its dark reptilian eyes move over me. It hisses and snaps

its jaws inches from my cheek. I crab crawl back. The chimera raises its armored tail again and brings it forward. The thorny end strikes my stomach. A volt of sudden, excruciating pain shoots through me, followed by a wave of nausea.

White stars flicker at the sides of my vision and everything tunnels to black.

Voices shout my name, but I can hardly hear them over the throbbing sensation in my head. I regain consciousness and look down. The stinger is lodged in my middle.

I try to scoot away, but when I do, a brand-new wave of pain hammers me. It feels like I'm burning from the inside out. Every breath brings more flaming stabs. I squeeze my eyes tight trying to shut it out. It doesn't help. As long as the stinger is in me, I won't find any relief. I bite down on my lower lip and stretch out my arms. I grasp the creature's tail. It's hard and smooth and hot to the touch. There's a sucking sound as I pull it out of my belly. The needlelike stinger is wet when it lifts away. I fall to the ground. In place of the sharp stabbing pain, there's a dull pulsing ache that spreads out from my stomach.

With its tail free, the chimera takes a step closer. Filmy drool slides down the edges of its jaws. Claws push into my shoulders, sharp, dry, and heavy. I say a silent prayer that there's some way out of this. The Komodo opens its mouth, and hot breath splays over my cheek. It reeks of sulfur. I fight back a shudder. The hybrid's forked yellow tongue slides out of its mouth, then swipes across my cheek. It suddenly recoils with a hiss like my skin burned its tongue. I glance at my arms and legs. They're still coated in borax, and there's an even thicker dusting on my hands. I inhale, then blow hard over my fingers. A puff of white powder flies directly in the creature's eyes. It recoils from me with a snarl.

I clutch my belly and stagger to my feet. I limp to the pile of spilled borax and grasp two handfuls. The chimera hisses again but holds its ground. I take another step closer, then fling the powder. It rears back, scratching at its face with its front legs. The borax sizzles on the lizard's scaly skin. It shudders but still doesn't run.

It takes all the strength I've got, but I lift the bag over my head and douse the contents onto the creature. At last, it curls its spiked tail up tight and retreats toward the woods.

I survey the thermal pool. The chimeras have surrounded Ezra, Nate, and Finn, but Maki and Jake have managed to escape. They're nearly to the path that leads away from the pool. But they're not alone. The mosquitoes have found them and are chasing them as they go. Maki swats them with the boom mic while Jake runs like wild, arms and legs flailing. After a moment, they all disappear down the trail.

I grab the nearly empty bag of borax and take off toward the rest of the mutant Komodos. But my legs don't move as fast as before. My head is fuzzy and my whole body feels sore and heavy. My guess is the hybrid injected some kind of venom when it stung me. I skirt around the thermal pool, avoiding the steamy bits of ground near the shore.

Nate, Ezra, and Finn have managed to climb onto a pile of debris made by one of the earthquakes. The hybrids are clawing at the rocks and broken tree limbs. It won't be long before they scale the barrier.

As I near the hybrids, their needle-tipped stingers rise. My side pulses at the sight. One takes a shuffling step my way. I dip my hand into the bag of borax. It's not enough and I know it.

"If you've got a plan, now's the moment to put it into action!" Finn cries out as one of the lizards rears up on its back legs, pressing its body against the rocks and coming dangerously close to him.

I sling all the remaining powder onto the closest lizards. It's nothing but a dusting. They hiss and shiver but hold their ground. It would take ten times the amount I've got to faze these guys.

One of the reptiles slashes a claw at a broken branch near Ezra's feet. "You did your best, Mags. Now you need to go. One of us has to get out of here alive."

"No!" I argue but fear and the pain in my side makes my head dizzy. I can't abandon them, but there's no way I'd survive even a second of combat with the chimeras.

I unzip my backpack with shaking hands, desperately searching for anything that can help. There's a flashlight, my journal, the maps. The brown paper sack from Penelope's sisters. I pause, remembering the slingshots Samantha said she added for our protection. I pull the sack out and scan the ground. But there aren't any rocks handy for ammo. Even if there were, I'm not sure they'd be enough to scare away Finn's mutants.

I blink and suddenly recall the incident with the hard candies and the coal snakes at the thermal pool. I'm not sure but . . . it just might work. I unwrap a piece of taffy and load it into the slingshot.

"Weaponized candy?" Nate asks dubiously.

I launch it at the closest hybrid. It lands on its back with a plink. The chimera shakes and the candy tumbles off. I slingshot another but the results aren't much better. Only the tiniest curl of black twists up.

Useless.

I'm about to toss the candies when Nate shouts, "Give them a chew. Mushy candy is way nastier than the dry stuff."

The chimeras are making progress ripping apart the barricade. In minutes, the lizards will reach the group. I glance at the reptiles' dusty scales. Nate has a point. At the pool, the hybrid was soaking wet.

I shove a few pieces in my mouth and chew fast and hard until the wad is soft and sticky, then yank it out and launch it in the slingshot. A bright blue glob splats on the nearest monster's snout. A few seconds later, the taffy goes from blue to black and starts to bubble and fester.

"Something's happening! Toss me a load and I'll pitch in!" Nate shouts.

"Me too!" Ezra adds.

"Coming up!" I throw a handful at each of them, plus the second slingshot. "Chew and fire!"

Nate and Ezra spew colorful mouthfuls onto the now-hissing chimeras while Finn wields the slingshot. In every place the chewed candies land, the blobs transform from rainbow shades to black steaming mounds within seconds. Smoke and a smell like burnt caramel rise in the air. Black carbon snakes twist and curl off every lizard.

I peer down into the bag. We're running low on ammo. We need to use the next few shots wisely. I study the lizards. The ones that have been hit in the eyes or mouth are moving a lot slower than those we pegged on the body.

"Aim for the face," I shout, and toss the final round of wrapped taffy to the others. They chew and carefully launch the wads. The candy blobs hit their marks. Jaws, eyes, and noses. The lizards writhe and hiss and at last slowly retreat. I slingshot one more squishy lump of taffy at a straggler, and it joins the others retreating to the thermal pool.

Nate grins. "We defeated reptilian monsters and I got to chow down on candy. Not a bad day all in all."

The lizards submerge themselves beneath the steaming water. With the coast clear, I hurry back to the mouth of the ravine. Dad's nearly to the top.

There's a staticky squawk. I glance at Finn's zapper lying in the dirt. It's silent. I listen a moment. It sounds like there's a voice mixed in with all the noise. I open my backpack.

It's the walkie-talkie. The batteries must have finally dried out. I lift it out of my bag and press the talk button. "Hello? Is anyone there?" I release the button.

"Magnolia! You're alive!" Gramma's voice bursts through. "Where are you? Where are the others? Are you okay?"

"Gramma!" I smile, glad to hear her voice again. "We're still in the park. We're at a pond . . . or actually a freshly formed thermal pool. I don't think it has a name, but there's a mud cauldron to our west and a fossil forest to the east." I glance at Nate and Ezra. "We're all together, but it hasn't been the easiest trip. I hope we'll be able to get back to you soon, but I'm not sure."

"What are you talking about? You think now that I've

found you I'm gonna give up?" Gramma's voice is ragged, like she's fighting off tears. "We'll be together by the end of the day, mark my words."

"We should get moving. It's still not safe here," Finn says.

"What's not safe?" Gramma's voice breaks in. "And who was that man? That didn't sound like your daddy."

"His name's Finn and he's a filmmaker, but the rest is a long story. We've gotta go, Gramma. We're still in a bit of a pickle."

"Keep your chin up, girl. I'll see you soon."

I tuck the walkie back in my bag, then peer into the ravine. Dad grips the rope tight and takes two more big steps. He's out at last. I wrap my arms around him and squeeze him tight. Pain shoots out from the site of the scorpion sting. Dad and I both release a groan at the same time. I pull back and look him over. "Are you okay?" I ask, wrapping one arm around my middle.

"Don't worry about me," he replies. "It's you I'm concerned about—you're hurt."

"I got stung by one of the creatures," I answer, my voice breaking. Now that Dad's here, all the fear and worry I've been holding in for days threatens to break free. I feel a prick behind my eyes and I blink. We're not out of this just yet. I've got to keep it together.

"We need to hurry," Finn warns.

"Who's that?" Dad asks, running his eyes over Finn suspiciously.

Finn avoids Dad's gaze. "I'm Finn Brody. I'm filming a documentary in the park."

"He's also the one responsible for the hybrids," I add.

A vein in Dad's forehead pulses, and he takes a limping step toward Finn. "You—"

Finn holds up both hands. "You can wring my neck later. Right now we need to move!"

"I don't think we're going anywhere soon." Ezra motions toward the trail. The sputtering geyser is now as tall as a house and as wide as a school bus. It completely blocks the path out of here.

"At least all the monsters have settled down," Nate says.

"About that." Finn eyes the thermal pool.

The water bubbles and Nate scowls. "Please tell me there's not something else down there."

Finn twists a metal stud in his ear nervously. "I may have overdone it with this next one."

CHAPTER TWENTY-FOUR

A translucent pink blob the size of a killer whale rockets out of the churning thermal pool. The creature is eyeless and gelatinous and resembles a massive, eight-legged hog. It wriggles and thrashes, making waves ripple over the pool.

Chills skitter down my arms. I've seen something like this before. In the Chimera Project files. "It's a moss piglet."

"A tardigrade?" Dad blinks as a funnel of steam blasts from the blobby creature's mouth.

"That thing got way bigger than I planned," Finn stammers apologetically.

"You really should've stuck to conspiracy theories," Nate says, and lifts his video camera. He pans over the tardigrade's wriggling belly, then suddenly raises the camera higher.

I glance up. A dark cloud moves our way. It hums with an obnoxious whine. "Not the mosquitoes again."

"I think we've got bigger worries than a few bugs," Dad says.

"These aren't your average insects," Nate replies.

"Why is every mutant in the park heading to this exact spot? It's like somebody announced a hybrid party and sent out invitations all over Yellowstone," Ezra complains.

Finn bites his lip. "This was going to be the site for my grand finale. I couldn't film without the chimeras. The thermal pool is a draw for the lizards, but just to be sure, I hid scented lures to attract each of the species."

"You were planning to film all of this?" Dad snaps, stomping toward Finn. "Did you even stop to think about all the ecosystems these mutants could destroy? Not to mention the people who'd be hurt?"

Finn slides a hand over his gelled-up hair. "I made some bad calls."

The mosquitoes buzz over the thermal pool, and the tardigrade twitches its head in their direction. The cloud of insects shifts away from the water and zooms our way.

"Unless we want to be unwilling blood donors we'd better get moving," I say. Dad wraps his arm around my side, and we limp toward the woods. The pain through my stomach is almost unbearable, and my legs feel wobbly under me. Nate, Ezra, and Finn start after us.

As the last few mosquitoes fly over the pool, the hulking tardigrade thrusts out of the water, like a seal beaching itself.

Sulfuric-smelling liquid splashes up, spraying us as we race by. Its mouth telescopes out three feet and it inhales a gerbil-size mosquito like it's slurping soda up through a straw.

Nate whistles. "Whoa, talk about potent bug control."

I wince as the still-fluttering insect travels through the transparent body of the tardigrade. A second later, another mosquito meets the same fate.

"This is incredible," Finn says, lingering near the pool. He's yanked out his video camera and is recording the whole scene. He turns our way, a wide grin spread across his face. "I know I should be sorry I made this guy, but just look at it!"

The tardigrade tilts its eyeless face in Finn's direction.

"You need to get out of there!" Nate calls.

Finn waves one hand dismissively. "Two more seconds."

But before he can turn and get even one more shot, the tardigrade extends its tubelike mouth and slurps Finn up whole.

CHAPTER TWENTY-FIVE

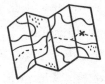

scream so loud it sounds like I've got a megaphone. Then I realize Ezra, Nate, and Dad are all screaming too. My whole body shakes. "It ate him! The tardigrade ate Finn!"

Dad turns to face the pool. "There might be a way to save him. If we can get to Finn before the tardigrade digests him, that is." Dad eyes the slimy beast. "I studied tardigrades a bit in college. They're tough, but not invincible. That thing can't handle being out of the water too long. It'll go into a state of cryptobiosis."

"What does that mean?" I ask.

"Moss piglets need a layer of moisture around their bodies at all times. If they don't have it, they curl up into dried-out balls called tuns. They can stay that way for years. That's why people sometimes say they're immortal. If I can keep it out of the water long enough, it should turn into a tun."

"But what about Finn? How will we get him out?" I

ask. Finn's made a lot of mistakes, but he doesn't deserve to be digested by his own creation.

Dad frowns. "I'll cross that bridge when I come to it."

"Be careful." Mist from the geyser blows through the air, sprinkling us in tiny droplets.

When Dad's a few yards away from the tardigrade, he raises his hands and hollers, "Come and get me!" The water bear flops toward him like a walrus doing tricks at Sea-World. Its telescopic mouth shoots out, and Dad jumps back. Just as he's about to run, something dark and green struts by the still-blasting geyser. There's no scorpion tail. Just a scaly reptilian body with slimy drool dripping from its mouth. It's Captain BiteyPants edging her way to Dad. At the same time, the tardigrade extends a clawed foot and inches closer.

"No," I breathe.

"We've gotta do something!" Ezra paces the dirt, looking panicked.

"We need to lead the tardigrade away from Dad. Once it dries up, we'll only have the Komodo dragon to worry about," I say, then hobble toward the moss piglet as fast as my beat-up body will carry me. Once I'm close enough, I wave my arms and yell, "Hey you, over here!"

"What are you doing, Maggie?" Dad calls. "Get outta here!"

"I'm buying you some time!" I bend and grab a stick, then launch it at the tardigrade's foot.

It lifts its wrinkly eyeless face in my direction, looking so ridiculously squishy and harmless that I almost forget it's just inhaled a man. I pick up another broken-off branch and toss it at the tardigrade's round side. Its snout twitches as though it's sniffing the air, though I'm not sure whether moss piglets even have a sense of smell. It doesn't matter. Judging by the way it's hustling in my direction, it definitely knows where I am.

As the remaining mosquitoes swarm through the air, Slither suddenly swoops low, flying with his mouth open wide. When he reaches the first oversize insect, he clamps his jaws shut and swallows it down.

I keep running and the tardigrade follows. It's faster than I would have thought a giant blob of jelly could be. Either that, or the hybrid's sting has made me a lot slower.

"Here, piggy, piggy, piggy," Nate sings out, coming along one side of the tardigrade. He jabs its middle with his fist.

"Look over here," Ezra taunts, and punches it on the other side.

The tardigrade stops chasing me and makes a U-turn for Nate and Ezra.

"Watch out!" I warn.

Nate and Ezra pivot and start to run the other way. I glance back in Dad's direction. He's headed toward the woods, but Captain BiteyPants is following close at his heels.

"I thought you said this thing was gonna dry out on land," Nate screeches.

"It will. I mean, it should," I say, pain blossoming through my stomach the faster I go. I glance at the creature. It doesn't look quite as shiny as before. "I think the running's helping. We've just got to get it a little drier."

"How are we supposed to do that? I don't see any industrial-size blow dryers lying around the place," Ezra pants.

There's no hair dryer, but we are getting close to the geyser. We can't run much farther in this direction without risking serious burns. I swallow and my throat feels dry and crackly. If only the tardigrade felt half as thirsty as me. My mind reels back to hot summer days riding my bike all over Shady Pines with Nate. We'd stop for salty snacks at Lenny's Supermarket. Afterward we'd both end up so thirsty, we'd chug entire bottles of water in a single gulp.

I spin to Nate, a half-formed idea ping-ponging through my head. "Do you have any snacks left in your bag?"

Ezra scowls. "You're hungry at a time like this?"

"It's for the tardigrade!" I call back.

The hefty beast makes wet slapping sounds on the dirt as it flops after us.

Nate yanks his bag open and pulls out a half-empty bag of Flamin' Hot Cheezy Poppers. "They're super stale. Even I won't touch 'em."

"Let's hope tardigrades aren't picky," I say.

Nate grabs a handful and tosses me the bag. We both throw out a few. The water bear immediately sucks up the bright orange puffs. I run farther from the pool and throw out more. The tardigrade keeps on chowing down. Its skin begins to crinkle like a peach left out in the sun too long.

"It's working! I should've known Cheezy Poppers would save my life one day." Nate beams.

The gelatinous monster belts out a grunt and releases a breath of hot steamy air. I throw more stale puffs, and it sucks them up. It shrinks again and its legs retract into its body, making it look more like a massive, super-squishy body pillow than a man-eating beast.

The tardigrade's skin is wrinkly and loose. A floppy whistling noise comes from its backside. The moss piglet is shrinking fast now, the wet trumpeting sound gets louder and the smell of sulfur is suddenly overpowering.

Nate jerks his head toward the creature and gags. "Oh, dang, tardigrade indigestion reeks."

There's a bubbly pop and another gurgly whistle. The

two jumbo mosquitoes zing out, looking like they were soaked in shiny green goo overnight. There's a flash of white-blond hair, and Finn shoots out of the back end of the tardigrade like a slimy cannonball. He flies a few feet, then crashes to the dirt with a soggy-sounding *kersplat*.

CHAPTER TWENTY-SIX

Finn lies limp on the ground. I look from Ezra to Nate. "Is he . . . dead?"

Ezra rushes to Finn's side and presses his fingers to his neck. "He's got a pulse . . . but he doesn't look so good."

On top of being coated in slippery green gunk, Finn's got a dozen swollen mosquito bites across his body.

Nate grimaces. "I guess being trapped in a piggy's belly with bloodsucking mutants isn't ideal."

With everyone out, the tardigrade folds in on itself like a deflated bounce house. When it finishes shrinking, it's small enough to fit in the palm of my hand. I skirt past the twitching mosquitoes, pick up the tardigrade, and slide it into my pocket.

Finn groans and tries to get to his feet, only to stumble back into the puddle of tardigrade goo. "I guess I deserve that," he mumbles.

The geyser has died down to a trickle, and the steamy

fog has cleared out. From the woods, I spot Dad stumbling our way. "Everybody all right?" he calls.

"You escaped the Komodo!" I say, and let out a tense breath.

"Actually, I didn't have much to do with that. The Komodo bumped into a wolf pack once we got to the woods. There were some hisses and growls, but I think they both decided it wasn't worth the trouble and went their separate ways."

Just then a whooshing sounds fills the air. I peer up. It's two helicopters circling over the thermal pool. A voice booms from the sky. "This is search and rescue. We're landing now!"

I clap my hands together. "We're getting out of here!"

The aircrafts veer toward the grassy area near the woods, and we race over to them. As they lower to the ground, the wind from the propellers whips my hair into knots.

I peek over my shoulder and notice Finn hasn't joined us. Instead, he's edging toward the trail. Ezra gives a low whistle and eyes the tree line. There's a crash of branches as Slither bursts through the woods. He swoops toward Finn, gulping a clump of mosquitoes on his way. Finn jumps back. The snake circles him, then wraps his long, thick tail around Finn's middle. "Let me go!" He screams and swats at the snake, but Slither only flicks his tongue out contentedly.

"Here, boy!" Ezra calls, and whistles again.

At that, Slither stretches out his wings and lifts Finn off the ground. He soars toward the helicopters, then uncoils his tail and deposits Finn in a crumpled heap. Slither sails higher, grazing the clouds above.

I turn to Ezra. "You taught him to fetch?"

Ezra grins. "He's a natural."

Finn rubs his head with one hand. "I regret adding golden retriever DNA to that one."

Two park rangers step out of the first helicopter—an older man with salt-and-pepper gray hair and a petite woman with freckles and warm brown eyes.

"Roy! Heather!" Dad waves.

The older man—Roy—squints at Dad. "Tommy? Is that you?"

Dad runs a hand across his stubbly chin. "I guess I'm looking a little disheveled these days."

Roy smiles. "We got a call from a Trudi Stone. Said her son and grandchildren were in a heap of trouble and that we'd better hurry out here."

"It's been a really strange week," Dad admits.

Roy places a hand on Dad's shoulder. "You and your family ready to get out of here?"

Dad nods. "I think we're all about as ready as humanly possible."

"Well, let's load up, then." Roy smiles.

Dad nods to Finn. "You'd better have him ride on his own. He's got a lot of explaining to do."

"What kind of explaining?" Heather asks.

Dad motions to a dark shape flying by a fluffy white cloud.

Roy and Heather gasp in unison. "Is that a dragon?"

"His name's Slither," Ezra answers. "He's a good boy."

"I—I see," Roy stammers.

As the other rangers escort Finn to their helicopter there's a thud, then another as Maki and Jake plop down to the ground. There's a flash of wings before Slither rises high in the sky and sails away.

Maki rubs her back. "Ouch."

Heather steps forward. "Do these two go in the other helicopter too?"

I reach out a hand to Maki and help her up. "Not her. She can ride with us."

Maki glances toward Finn as the rangers seat him in the second aircraft. "Thanks for the offer, but I intend to give Finn a piece of my mind."

"Well, all right." Heather smiles.

In a few minutes, we're all loaded up and ready for takeoff. Roy rides in the front with the pilot and the rest of us take the back. As we lift into the air, I peer down at the thermal pool. Wisps of fog swirl over its surface, and I can just make out the outline of the hatchlings. They're swimming together in an unbroken line, making soft ripples as they glide across the water.

We fly over trees and rivers and trails. All over the park, there's evidence of the damage caused by the earthquakes. The helicopter takes a turn, and the trees thin out. "What do you think will happen to all the chimeras Finn made?" I ask.

Ezra frowns. "They can't stay in the park. That's for sure. They're too dangerous . . . and weird. Visitors would freak out."

I study Ezra's face and consider what he said about not knowing where he fit in anymore. "Yellowstone might not be the best spot for them, but that doesn't mean there's not a place for them somewhere. With a little time, people might be more accepting than you'd think."

"Maybe so," Ezra says thoughtfully.

I shift my gaze to Dad. "And while we're thinking about rehoming Finn's creations, we can't forget the world's largest tardigrade." I reach into my pocket and hand Dad the tun. "But no rush. From what I hear, this thing can hold on the shelf for a while. Just remember, don't get it wet."

He peers down at the tardigrade shriveled into a tight, dry ball. "Don't worry. It'll be on a strict no-liquid diet," he says, and smiles.

Every part of my body hurts, and I don't know when I last showered or ate a meal without worrying that I might be eaten next. But somehow, I'm alive, and so are Ezra and Nate and Dad. We're battered and bruised and maybe a little warier of lizards than we were before, but we made it through. For a while, it felt like I didn't know who anybody was anymore. But we pulled together. We're a team. In good times and bad. If this trip helped me remember that, it was worth at least a couple of jumbo mosquito bites.

The helicopter makes a slow turn, and we fly over the edges of town. I spot something white and fluttery down below. It's the chuckwagon. Penelope and her little sisters stand in front of the wagon, hugging a man and woman. I smile. They found their parents after all. At the sound of the propeller, they all look up. I reach my arm out the door and wave. Penelope and her sisters wave back.

I lean my head against the seat as we soar over a parking lot filled with a convoy of jeeps and police cars. The helicopter lowers to the ground. "This is it. We made it," Dad says.

The other ranger opens the aircraft door. "It's time we get you all some medical care. But first, there's somebody who's been dying to see you."

As we step onto the asphalt, I catch a glimpse of fluffy silver hair and flamingo-pink shorts before I'm wrapped up in a big hug. "Not too tight, Gramma. It's been a rough few days," I say, and breathe in the familiar smell of gardenia perfume. I relax into her arms, letting all the worries of the last week ebb away.

When I pull back, I see Gramma's eyes are rimmed with red, and her cheeks are wet. "You wanna tell me about a rough few days? I've been worried sick about all of you! I haven't slept a wink." She kisses my forehead. "Oh my, I'm so glad you're safe, my girl."

Dad and Ezra step out of the helicopter next, and Gramma ambushes them just as fast. "You're alive!" She laughs. "Hallelujah!"

CHAPTER TWENTY-SEVEN

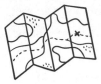

We spend the next three days getting treated at the local hospital. The doctors are all kinda creeped out by the sting on my belly. I guess I'm the first patient they've treated for mutant venom. They also confirmed Nate's bite was from a Komodo dragon and not a wolf. They said the antibiotics Maki gave him probably saved his life.

While we've been resting up, Dad's put in lots of calls and found a reptile rehabilitation center not far from Yellowstone. A team's already transported Captain BiteyPants and her hatchlings there. The tardigrade is going to a natural history museum, and the jumbo mosquitoes and jackalopes are staying in Yellowstone for now. Though rangers are warning visitors to wear bug spray and never feed any bunnies, no matter how cute or harmless they seem.

Maki stopped by the hospital yesterday. She said Finn confessed to using modified CRISPR-Cas9 and the gene gun to make his mutants. He took all the blame and left Jake out of the whole thing. Investigators found his lab and watched all his videos. Some people are pretty impressed with his work, but a lot more are angry. He might be in hot water for a while.

After I finish what I hope is my last hospital meal for a very long time, I change out of my gown and into the fresh clothes Gramma brought by this morning. Once I'm discharged, we load up in Dad's car and head back to his cabin. There's still plenty of broken trees and bits of rubble from the quakes around his place. But the air is filled with the smell of pine, and the sun is warm on my cheeks. We grill hamburgers and roast marshmallows and try to stuff all the things we missed out on into our final evening here.

In the morning, as we pack our bags into Gramma's car, Slither hovers over the cabin, his wide wings beating the air.

Ezra waves. "Take it easy, man." The snake soars above the canopy and Ezra sighs.

I lean against a tree trunk. "You're going to miss him, aren't you?"

He nods. "I'll never forget him. He taught me a lot."

"Like how to eat rodents from the air?" I grin.

Ezra laughs and pushes his hands into his pockets. "Like it's okay if I'm a little different. I mean, Slither is super weird, but he's also pretty much the coolest creature I've ever met. When we first got here, I was sure nobody would understand all the things running through my head. But I think maybe I was the one making it hard, not everybody else."

I smile. "I never thought I'd get used to a snake with wings, but now it seems totally normal. Maybe more snakes should have wings. He could start a trend."

Dad hops down the porch steps, carrying Gramma's suitcase. "One Slither might be all the world can handle."

We laugh and I wrap my arms around his neck and give him a final hug. "See you at Thanksgiving?" I ask.

"Thanksgiving? I'm not waiting that long. I'm driving down for Labor Day and Halloween, too. Then Christmas and New Year's and every other holiday I can think of until we're all together under one roof again," Dad says. "I'm gonna be around so much, you'll be sick of me."

I poke his side. "Only if you try to do the cooking. Canned meat just isn't my thing."

"I second that," Ezra says. "But come around as much as you want. We won't get sick of you." Dad grins and pulls him in close.

Once the last bag is loaded, Gramma shuts the trunk. "Who's ready to hit the road? I've got Tupperware containers packed with old-fashioned popcorn balls and another with pimento cheese sandwiches."

At the mention of cheese, Nate bolts to the back seat. "I'm ready!"

As we drive away from Dad's cabin, Ezra dozes off and Nate pulls out his camcorder to scroll through videos. "We've got loads of footage to post when we get back home."

"Think any of them will go viral?" I ask, nibbling on a gooey bit of popcorn.

"I sure hope so. I filled up the entire memory card while we were here."

We pass the curving green waters of the Firehole River, and Nate suddenly smashes his face against the back-seat window. "Did you just see that, Mags?"

"What is it?" I shift my eyes in his direction.

There's a flash of furry brown moving through the trees and long arms swinging low. My eyes meet Nate's. "He's real!"

"What are you two hollering about?" Gramma asks, peering through the rearview mirror.

"Bigfoot!" we squeal in unison.

AUTHOR'S NOTE

I hope you've enjoyed Maggie and Nate's latest adventure. As in the first book, some elements of the story are based on real science while others are purely fictional.

Yellowstone National Park, the story's setting, is a **true geological wonder.** The park is home to more than ten thousand hydrothermal features and has the most active geysers in the world. It's a vast wilderness occupying nearly thirty-five hundred square miles across three states. As in the book, **earthquake swarms** do occur in the park, but most are so small you wouldn't notice them. Both the thermal features and the earthquakes are caused by the active supervolcano lying beneath the surface of the national park. But have no fear, geologists predict the volcano won't erupt anytime soon.

While stranded in Yellowstone, Maggie and Nate discover a **secret laboratory** filled with strange specimens, like the petri dish of **thermophilic bacteria.** Many real-life thermophiles thrive in the hot, acidic waters of Yellowstone's hydrothermal pools. And while scientists haven't used them to bioengineer lizards that can swim in near-boiling water, they have harnessed extremophile DNA to help ice cream stay smooth as it freezes and to produce grain crops that are more resilient to bad weather.

The book's namesake, the **Komodo dragon,** likely won't be visiting Yellowstone anytime soon—and that's a good thing as the reptile is a truly fierce predator. On top of being the world's largest lizard, it's also equipped with sharklike teeth, a venomous bite, and an impressive suit of armor made from tiny bones beneath its scales. Even so, if the fearsome reptile got into a tussle with a giant, nearly indestructible tardigrade, it remains to be seen who would emerge the victor.

Tardigrades, also known as water bears or moss piglets, are tiny eight-legged creatures that have been found all over the planet from frozen Antarctic glaciers to steamy lava fields. They've survived the vacuum of space, high doses of radiation, and the crushing pressure of the deep oceans. Like the oversize specimen in this book, real-life tardigrades possess a ravenous appetite but require moisture to stay mobile. Otherwise, they shrivel up into a dehydrated ball called a **tun.** In this dormant state, tardigrades can go decades without food or water. But with only a few drops of water, water bears can come back to life in a matter of hours. That would certainly make it a tough opponent for any Komodo dragon.

Lastly, **CRISPR technology**—the science used to genetically modify animals in the book—is real, and so is the gene gun, also known as a **biolistic particle delivery system,** Finn Brody uses to deliver new DNA to his creatures. But neither can create anything as extreme as a snake with wings or a lizard with a scorpion tail . . . at least not yet. However, scientists have used CRISPR to produce beagle puppies with double the amount of muscles. There's even a **team** at Harvard University working on bringing the **woolly mammoth back from extinction** by combining mammoth DNA with that of an Asian elephant. Imagine seeing one of those in the wild someday! Maggie and Nate would definitely want to have their cameras handy to catch it all on film.